Vampire City

also by Paul Féval
translated, annotated and introduced by
Brian Stableford

Knightshade

The Vampire Countess

Vampire City

(La Ville-Vampire)

by
Paul Féval

translated, annotated and introduced by
Brian Stableford

A Black Coat Press Book

Acknowledgements: I am indebted to Xavier Legrand-Ferron-nière, who located a copy of the Marabout edition of *La Ville-Vampire* for me, and to Robert Morgan, whose Sarob Press provided the translation with its first home, thus encouraging me to go on and translate *Knightshade* and *The Vampire Countess*. I should also like to thank Jane Stableford and David McDonnell for proofreading the typescript.

Visit our website at www.blackcoatpress.com

Table of Contents

Introduction

La Ville-Vampire was first published in book form in 1875, although internal evidence suggests that it must have been written eight years earlier, probably for serialization in a French newspaper. It is the third novel Paul Féval had written which employs the notion of vampirism, and by far the most extravagant. Like its immediate predecessor *Le Chevalier Ténèbre* (1860; tr. as *Knightshade*), it is an alloy of comedy and horror fiction, but whereas *Knightshade* was framed according to the "Galland formula" of tales nested within tales, *Vampire City* is a parody of the classic Gothic novel, which appropriates as its heroine the most successful of all the authors in that genre, Ann Radcliffe.

The flood of imitations which Mrs. Radcliffe's novels had provoked at the beginning of the 19th century had already begun to die away when she died in 1823, but the genre was to enjoy two further leases on life in England. The first came courtesy of the "bluebooks" which packaged condensed versions of the most famous Gothic novels and crude imitations thereof in cheap formats, usually retailing at a shilling. (Bound books usually retailed at 10s 6d, and novels were conventionally issued in three volumes to suit the convenience of the circulating libraries.) The second came with a new wave of part-work publications and cheap periodicals launched in the 1840s, which extended the reading habit to the working classes and became known as "penny dreadfuls." These were supplemented in the 1850s by single-volume cardboard-covered "railway novels" which provided cheap distraction for the middle-class traveler. Again, the classics were reprinted for a new generation and again they spawned new and even cruder imitations. It was this third flood of Gothics old and new–and especially the final vulgarization of the form– that prompted Féval's parody.

At the time of its first publication, the hybrid horror/comedy genre to which *Vampire City* belongs hardly existed, and Féval may be credited with its invention. It was not a great success in its own day, but now that comic books and movies have made horror/comedy a familiar genre it is difficult to write "traditional" horror stories–especially those with Gothic elements–without a gloss of satirical humor. The existence of the modern subgenre facilitated a paperback reprint *Vampire City* in 1972, issued by the Belgian publisher Marabout in the same volume as *Knightshade*. That reprint was sufficiently well-received to play a significant part in prompting Alberto Manguel and Gianni Guadalupi to compile *The Dictionary of Imaginary Places* (1980)–an inspiration noted in their introduction.

The spread of gruesome horror motifs from 18-rated movies to the universally-accessible medium of television has resulted in the restoration of a certain calculated coyness to the presentation of Gothic imagery, which is routinely combined with a calculatedly light note of stylized irony. With the aid of hindsight, we can easily see in *Vampire City* the ultimate literary ancestor of the popular television show *Buffy the Vampire-Slayer*. Although the fictitious "Anne Radcliffe" is not permitted by her gentlemanly author actually to slay any vampires with her own hand, she is nevertheless the prime mover of the expedition to the Vampire City of Selene; she watches with a distinctly proto-feminist fascination as the Irish hero carefully excises the heart from the breast of a comatose vampire.

By virtue of this happy coincidence, the baroque humor of *Vampire City* is more likely to appeal to modern English and American readers than it could have done had a translation followed hot on the heels of its first appearance in France. Even the stream of sly insults leveled at the English can be easily laughed off by the contemporary English reader, because they clearly apply to the Victorians and not to us. If the timing of this translation is in any way miscalculated, it can only be because the deluge of vampire stories launched in the late 1970s by the best-selling works of Anne Rice (the Ann Radcliffe of the 20th century!) has been so prolific as to have run itself almost to exhaustion in a mere twenty years–but one can easily argue that its overworked state only renders it all the more ripe for cavalier parody.

Paul Féval's biography and importance as a pioneer of popular fiction are extensively detailed in the introductions and afterwords to the two companion volumes to *Vampire City*, *The Vampire Countess* and *Knightshade*. It seems reasonable, therefore, to concentrate the bulk of this introduction on the career of Ann Radcliffe, and her significance as a Gothic novelist.

Radcliffe was the most popular British author of the 1790s, not merely in Britain but throughout continental Europe, where she became the most widely-translated English author of that era. Her first two novels were both issued anonymously; the Scotland-set *The Castles of*

Athlin and Dunbayne (1789), was a slender and rather weak melodrama but *A Sicilian Romance* (1790), although it was not much longer, presented a far more striking story cast solidly in what would soon come to be recognized as the Gothic mold.

The central element of the Gothic formula is a huge and ancient house, usually a crumbling Medieval castle whose battlements and narrow windows provide reminders of an ancient insecurity which has supposedly been overtaken by modern civilization. It is invariably surrounded by a wild and precipitous landscape and usually sits atop a labyrinthine network of cellars, dungeons and caves. All the barbarities which it symbolizes, thinly covered by a superficial veneer of civilization, are mirrored in the character of its master, a male villain whose charm and erudition masks fervent ambition. He will stop at nothing to protect his mastery, and this routinely involves the necessity to murder, imprison or marry the true heir to "his" estate–a process which routinely involves the separation of young lovers. His avarice is often combined with lust, which is frequently incestuous, and the mocking politeness which routinely cloaks his insidious threat is often betrayed by environmental disturbances which range from curious weather phenomena to all manner of visual and auditory apparitions.

Despite his ruthlessness, the average Gothic villain is often inefficient in disposing of his victims, who are frequently mislaid for ten or twenty years, sometimes being sold to gypsies, kidnapped by brigands or stolen by pirates. They are often raised in ignorance of their true identity before some freak of chance lets the secret loose. Although it is not, strictly speaking, part of the fundamental recipe, it is also worth nothing that the Gothic formula's obsession with aristocratic inheritance is routinely counterpointed with a depiction of the servant class which is almost comic; when Gothic novels were adapted for lower class readers, the roles of these awkwardly-constructed menials were often padded out and made more heroic.

Although Horace Walpole's *The Castle of Otranto* (1764) is nowadays recognized as the original template from which the classic Gothics were stamped, it was not a particularly influential work in the 18th century, partly because it was so obviously a joke. Although some modern critics have tried to affiliate William Beckford's gaudy Oriental fantasy *Vathek* (1786)–which is even more sarcastic–to the Gothic tradition, the quarter-century following the publication of *The Castle of Otranto* actually produced only two significant novels which employed its formula more earnestly, both of them written by women. Both were careful to eliminate the supposedly-archaic supernatural elements of Walpole's plot, but they greatly exaggerated and extrapolated the sense of veiled threat to which their heroines were subjected. These two novels were Clara Reeve's *The Champion of Virtue* (1777; better known as *The Old English Baron*) and Sophia Lee's *The Recess* (1783-85). Ann Radcliffe read both of them, and was for some time a near neighbor of Sophia Lee in Bath (causing some later speculation as to whether she might have attended the school run by Sophia and her sister Harriet).

Radcliffe took from these examples the firm resolution that all apparently-supernatural events in her works must eventually be given a rational explanation–an aspect of her work which Féval casually disregards, except for a couple of sly asides–but she certainly did not underestimate the power of apparently supernatural events to reflect and symbolize the terror to which her heroines were reduced by the interest shown in them by urbane but malevolent older males. She became expert in the art of impregnating descriptions of architecture, landscape and polite behavior with oblique menace.

Having undertaken a trial run in *A Sicilian Romance*, Ann Radcliffe allowed her imagination full rein in *The Romance of the Forest* (1791), the first book to which she attached a signature and the first which employed a charismatically sinister villain, the Marquis de Montalt. The novel's popularity was such that she was offered 500 pounds–an unprecedented sum–for the right to publish *The Mysteries of Udolpho* (1794), which became a runaway bestseller and the inspiration for a flood of imitations. Its villain, Montoni, became the archetype of his species. So successful was the novel, in fact, that the publisher broke his own record by offering 800 pounds for *The Italian* (1797; sometimes reprinted under its original subtitle, *The Confessional of the Black Penitents*), in which the villain, Father Schedoni, shelters beneath the protective disguise of a man of the cloth all the viciousness and violence of the ancient Inquisition. All sophisticated readers agreed that he was a more impressive figure than the infinitely less subtle villain of Matthew Gregory Lewis's *The Monk* (1796), but unsophisticated ones were not so sure. Lewis borrowed extensively from contemporary German tales of terror–which were not in the least ashamed of graphic supernatural devices–so *The Monk* achieved the greater *succès de scandale* and became the more powerful influence on downmarket Gothics. Although it was Ann Radcliffe's works which first gripped the imagination of Catherine Morland, the innocent heroine of Jane Austen's *Northanger Abbey*, she–like the public at large–was beguiled soon afterwards by "horrid novels" soon afterwards by "horrid novels" of a more garish Germanic stripe.

In the same year as *The Italian*, Mrs. Radcliffe published a version of journals she had kept during her one and only expedition to continental Europe, *A Journey Made in the Summer of 1794 through Holland and the Western Frontier of Germany With a Return Down the Rhine, To Which are Added Observations of a Tour of the Lakes*. Presumably, she might have obtained 1,000 pounds for her next novel, but she did not; she published nothing more during her lifetime, although she did not die until 1823, when she was killed by one of the fits of asthma to which she had became increasingly subject. She must have known by then that she had conferred such awesome power on her villains as to inspire Lord Byron to employ them as role models, but we can only speculate as to what she made of that perverse appropriation.

Considering that she was so outstanding a figure, it is surprising that nothing at all was known to her contemporaries of Ann Radcliffe's private life. In spite of intense curiosity, no biographical details were published until a notice appeared in the *Annual Biography and Obituary* in 1824; it was unsigned but was certainly written by her husband William Radcliffe. William also helped to prepare the posthumous publication of the novel *Gaston de Blondeville* in 1826, along with some examples of her poetry and a "memoir" by Thomas Noon Talfourd, which added a few more biographical details provided–or at least supervised–by William. All the hard data included in Sir Walter Scott's *Memoir of Mrs. Ann Radcliffe* and subsequent biographical commentaries are taken from these two sources.

Despite the fact that Ann had long kept a journal and was said to have written a good deal for her personal amusement after ceasing to publish, so little material remained a generation later that Christina Rossetti, having set out to write Ann's biography, was forced to give up for lack of material. This has caused some modern commentators to observe, wryly, that there is no other British popular author since Shakespeare whose personal affairs are so little-documented.

William Radcliffe's obituary of Ann gives absolutely no indication of how his wife came to write the kind of books she wrote, and none as to why she quit while she was so far ahead of her field. Given that he was presumably partly responsible for the dearth of surviving documents, his comments may seem to the modern reader to be calculated to maintain a veil of secrecy. It is in this historical context that the modern reader needs to set Féval's calculatedly frivolous speculations about the nature of Mrs. Radcliffe's inspiration and his vividly excessive caricature of the formula that she brought to its peculiar perfection.

The one aspect of Féval's career relevant to *Vampire City* that was not covered in sufficient detail in the introductions to the earlier volumes is his relationship with English publishers. Mention was made in the introduction to *The Vampire Countess* of his resentment of George Reynolds' rival version of *The Mysteries of London*, and it is possible that Féval would be much better known today had he made friends with Reynolds and used Reynolds' publishing operations as a conduit for authorized translations of his works. Instead, *Vampire City* opens with the complaint that the English were habitual literary thieves, ripping off other people's ideas

14

wholesale. Given Féval's own propensity for pastiche, this may seem akin to the pot calling the kettle black– and the complaint is slightly tongue-in-cheek–but there is no doubt that English and American attitudes to what would now be called "intellectual property" were still a trifle piratical in the mid-19th century. It is by no means easy to determine the exact extent to which Féval was a victim of such malpractice, but there seems little doubt that he was a significant victim of such piracy.

Wholesale literary theft by British publishers began in the late 1830s, when–as the text of *Vampire City* acknowledges–their leading victim was Charles Dickens. The popular success of part-work editions of Dickens' novels inspired dozens of plagiarisms, laying the commercial foundations for the ultra-cheap part-works that quickly came to be known as "penny dreadfuls." The publishers of penny dreadfuls expanded in the 1840s into the production of new editions of Gothic horror stories and imitations thereof, the most famous neo-Gothic serials written for that format being James Malcolm Rymer's *Varney the Vampyre*, G. W. M. Reynolds' *Wagner the Wehr-Wolf* and Thomas Peckett Prest's *The String of Pearls* (the last-named being the story of Sweeney Todd, the "demon barber of Fleet Street"). All of these were in production in 1846-47, the years when penny dreadful publishing reached the peak of its popularity and notoriety. It was presumably works of this caliber which Féval had in view when he planned his parody–and Reynolds' involvement must have caught his attention particularly.

An amazingly prolific author and publisher, George William MacArthur Reynolds (1814-79) was a key figure in the development of penny periodicals. Initially destined for a military career, he left Sandhurst rather abruptly in 1830 and removed himself to France, where

15

he lived for the next seven years, first in Calais and later in Paris. In 1835, he was a co-founder of an expatriate newspaper, *The London and Paris Courier*, and published his first book, *The Youthful Imposter*, whose failure apparently reduced him to penury and forced his return to London, where he became editor of the *Monthly Magazine*. Although Reynolds left Paris before Féval arrived, it is possible that the two men met at some point, and they must at least have had acquaintances in common.

Reynolds was one of the first writers to see the commercial potential of pastiches of popular writers, and he serialized his own *Pickwick Abroad: or The Tour in France* in the *Monthly Magazine* in 1837-38. He also published a series of studies reprinted as *The Modern Writers of France* (1839) before quarrelling with his employers and quitting the magazine at the end of 1838. He published a couple more pastiches but kept a relatively low profile until 1844, when he began to produce a penny part-work for the publisher George Vickers which was to become a huge bestseller and the foundation-stone of a spectacular career as an editor and astonishingly prolific producer of popular fiction. That part-work was *The Mysteries of London*.

It is hardly surprising that Féval thought that his own serial–begun earlier and still running, in a periodical whose title had been copied by Reynolds–was the inspiration for Reynolds' *Mysteries of London*, and that the idea had been blatantly stolen. Reynolds could, and presumably would, have defended himself by pointing out that he and Féval had both been commissioned by editors and that their employers had taken the fundamental inspiration from Eugène Sue–and he would undoubtedly have added the observation that London was,

16

after all, the capital of England, and that its mysteries were undoubtedly better-known to an Englishman than a Frenchman, even if the Englishman had spent so much time in France. This apparent theft was, however, to be followed by numerous real ones.

The original British Museum catalog has no entry for Paul Féval and the Wellesley Index of leading Victorian periodicals includes only one (presumably authorized) translation of his work–an article in *Bentley's Miscellany*. Although the copyright library at the British Museum received no 19th century British editions of Féval's work, one London-published work is contained in the National Union Catalog: an 1846 edition of *The Loves of Paris*, published by the same George Vickers for whom Reynolds had written *The Mysteries of London*. This must have been pirated, and there seem to have been numerous other pirate editions of Féval's works within the twilight world of the penny periodicals. Louis James' study *Fiction for the Working Man* (1963) only mentions one–George Pierce's edition of *The Midnight Reckoning*–but a list of translations into various languages compiled by Yves Meinnel as an addendum to his essay in *Paul Féval: Romancier Populaire* claims that there were British editions of *Le Loup Blanc* (*The White Wolf*) in 1845, *Le Mendiant Noir (The Black Mendicant*) in 1848, *Le Bossu* (*The Hunchback*) and *Beau Démon* (*Handsome Devil*, aka *Bel Demonio*) in 1863, *Le Fils du Diable* (*The Son of the Devil*) in 1880 and a translation of *La Fée des Grèves* (*The Fairy of the Shores*) whose date is unknown. All of these must have been pirated if they do exist.

The London Library collection includes an 1882 Vizetelly edition of an English translation of *Le Fils du Diable*, entitled *The Three Red Knights*; or, *The Broth-*

ers' Vengeance, which might be a reprint if Meinnel's date is correct. Four of the five books published in English in the USA which are listed in the National Union Catalog are probably also pirate editions; these are: *The Black Mendicant* (1847), *The White Wolf* (c. 1850), *"I Am Here!" The Duke's Motto* (an 1863 translation of *Le Bossu*, reprinted in 1887 as *"I Am Here!" Lagardère; or, The Hunchback of Paris*) and *The Golden Daggers* (1864). *The Jesuits* (1878; a tr. of *Les Jesuites*, 1877), being a translation of a pious tract, is far more likely to have been authorized. There may well have been other translations from Féval in British and American periodicals.

Given the extent of this catalog, it is hardly surprising that Féval felt some resentment against British publishers, although his comments about loopholes in International Copyright Law are a trifle mischievous (the "fair use" clause does not license plagiarism and the penny dreadful publishers who continued pirating after the act was signed were quite simply–and quite consciously–breaking the law). In fact, Féval's objections in *Vampire City* seem reasonably good-humored, and the novel's final wry twist is calculated to take some of the sting out of the sly put-downs to which the English are continually subjected in the course of the plot. The fundamentally-Anglophile Féval must have recognized that he and George Reynolds had a great deal in common in addition to being chroniclers of the mysteries of London, at least until Féval's conversion to zealous Catholicism (after *Vampire City* was written) set him firmly against the kind of radical freethought of which Reynolds was a tireless champion.

Vampire City is now in the public domain, so the following translation is no act of piracy. Indeed–as

Féval's work continually observes, in comparing his present with the past eras recreated in his novels–the passage of time changes all things, perennially providing us with new perspectives. I would like to think that in preparing this series of translations I am paying Paul Féval a long-overdue compliment and doing him the favor of adding my voice to a growing chorus of appreciation of his sterling efforts in the invention of popular fiction. I hope that if he had been able to imagine, in 1867, that his three vampire novels would be in print in English in the early years of the 21st century, he would have been delighted.

Brian Stableford

PART ONE

Prologue

There are many people in England, especially English women, who are appalled when they are told of the acts of blatant piracy to which French writers are subjected in England. Her Most Gracious Majesty Queen Victoria once signed a treaty with France with the laudable intention of putting an end to these oft-repeated thefts. The treaty is very well made, except that it contains one tiny clause that renders its terms illusory. Her Most Gracious Majesty, in effect, forbids her loyal subjects to appropriate our plays, books and so on, but she permits them to make that which she is pleased to call a "fair imitation"[1].

This is nice, but not honest. My dear and excellent friend Charles Dickens said to me one day, by way of apology: "I am not much better protected than you. When I go to London, if I happen to have an idea about my person, I lock my notecase, put it in my pocket and keep both hands upon it. It is stolen anyway."

The simple fact is that the "fair imitation" clause dangles temptation before subtle pickpockets.

Mr. Dickens' charming friend, Lady B*** of Shr*** House [2], has repeatedly asked me the same

---

[1] (see Notes page 195.)

question every time that I have had the pleasure of seeing her during the last twenty years: "Why don't you get your own back by stealing from the English?"

"It is certainly not that there is nothing in your books that would be worth stealing, Madame," I used to reply, "but I fear that our national character will not allow Frenchmen to indulge even in fair trickery."

That response caused Milady to burst out laughing. She even went so far as to recommend some suitable candidates to me... but hush! I have a tale to tell.

One morning late last year, Milady generously sprang a surprise on me.

"I am taking you away," she said. "I have arranged everything with your dear wife. We depart this evening."

"And we are going...?"

"To my place."

"In the Rue Castiglione?"

"No, to Shr*** House in Staffordshire."

"I don't know about that!"

The weather was atrocious. If snow was falling and the wind was howling even in Paris, how rough would the crossing from Calais to Dover be?

Milady, brought up on Byron, was a lover of storms. "Don't be put off," she said, "just because you're afraid of catching cold. I have figured out a way to return, at a single stroke, everything that England has stolen from you. It's a red-hot opportunity. Mr X*** and Miss Z*** are already on the track, and besides, at Miss 97's age one simply doesn't have the time to hang about."

Mr X*** and Miss Z*** are two of the most sensational English novelists, always on the lookout for a good idea for a story. I asked for further details, but Milady refused to explain, being content to employ her extraordinary God-given eloquence to excite my curiosity.

"Do you trust Walter Scott?" she asked. "He was a passionate admirer of *The Mysteries of Udolpho* and wrote a biography of Mrs. Anne Radcliffe. Think of it: Walter Scott! Dickens himself once went to see Miss 97–in those days she was called Miss 94, but she changes her name every year on Christmas Day. I'm well acquainted with her stories, but this one is so extraordinary..."

I gave in, of course. We set out immediately. The crossing was hideous; it will haunt my dreams forever. All the demons of the air and sea played with that ferry as if it were a rubber balloon. The next day, we took a train from London to the northwest and stayed the night in Stafford. The day after that, Milady's landau conveyed us over a snow-covered plain into the hills on the borders of Shropshire. That evening, we dined at Milady's house.

This was what I had found out during the journey:

We were in the native region of the Mr. and Mrs. Ward who were the parents of the woman who was to become famous as Anne Radcliffe [3]. Miss 97–who was only three years short of her hundredth birthday–was a second cousin of the Wards. She lived in a cottage in the hills, just over three miles from Milady's house. This cottage had long been the residence of her illustrious kinswoman.

I do not use the word *illustrious* lightly and I am prepared to defend it against any claim of exaggeration. The fame of Anne Radcliffe was worldwide at one time, and her dark tales obtained a height of fashionability that our most successful contemporaries have been unable to equal. It was said that she cast her spell on cottage and country house alike. *The Mysteries of Udolpho* went through two hundred editions in England. In France the book was translated several times over, and one of those versions was reprinted forty times in Paris. Nor was it a brief infatuation; by now the fever has calmed somewhat, but *The Mysteries of Udolpho* and *The Confessional of the Black Penitents* still terrify thousands of young imaginations everywhere.

Now, Miss 97 knew of a personal experience of Anne Radcliffe, which Anne Radcliffe herself had told to her some seventy years previously. It was widely rumored in the region that it was this episode that had turned the placid and rather cheerful temperament of Anne Radcliffe into the terrible gloom that characterized her work.

Walter Scott had had a vague inkling of this story, as is evidenced by a letter which he wrote on May 3, 1821 to his editor Constable, which contains this passage:

"As regards the manuscript of the *Life of Anne Radcliffe*, I shall delay its delivery until after my next interview with Miss Jebb, from which I hope to extract some useful and very interesting items of information. This woman is, it is said, the custodian not merely of a secret but of a 'significant curiosity' which will inject considerable interest into our story..."

This Miss Jebb was none other than our own Miss 97, who had now added forty-five years to the date of Scott's letter [4]. Like all the English, she had a weakness for the nobility, and Milady had persuaded her to put off Miss Z*** and Mr X*** because they were writers of a "common" stripe.

After breakfast on the day after our arrival, which was cold and grey, Milady invited me to climb into a carriage. We traveled for half an hour, then pulled up at a green-painted wooden gate which served as the entrance to a little old house, whose appearance was thoroughly respectable. The hills loomed above it on three sides, but the open countryside to the south was pleasant.

We were admitted to a parlour whose size was appropriate to the smallness of the house. Several portraits hung on the walls, mounted in decoratively gilded wooden frames.

A tall and lean old woman was sitting in the corner beside the stove. She seemed to me to be formed like a certain kind of bird, to which I couldn't put a name although I was sure I had once seen a regal specimen in a taxidermist's shop. Her nose had a razor's sharpness and her round eyes seemed half-asleep.

"How are you getting on, my dear Jebb?" Milady asked, affectionately.

"Not badly–and your Ladyship?"

I looked around the room to see who had spoken. There were only the three of us. Miss 97 was a natural ventriloquist. Her voice had circled around us and was heard as if from behind. She must have lost her looks a long time before, but she had conserved her strength well enough.

When Milady had introduced me, we sat down. The voice of Miss 97, resounding as if from the other side of the parlor, addressed me benevolently. "The Frenchman, monsieur, is brave and clever, the Italian wily, the Spaniard cruel, the German dull, the Russian brutal, the Englishman happy and remarkable in his generosity. *She* liked Frenchmen."

Miss 97 lifted her eyes to the ceiling as she pronounced the word *She*–which, upon her lips and punctuated with pious regard, always referred to Anne Radcliffe. The quotation which preceded it, with which I was unfortunately unfamiliar, was from *A Sicilian Romance*, the second novel which *She* had written.

"What style!" exclaimed Milady. "And what profundity!"

"I am honored," Miss 97 replied, "to express my gratitude to Your Ladyship."

From her overcoat, which she had removed on entering the cottage, Milady took a parcel containing four duodecimo volumes. It was the French translation of Sir Walter Scott's *Biographies of Famous Writers*, published in Paris by Charles Gosselin in 1820.

"You see that *She* is loved in France," said Milady earnestly, as she opened the volume which contained the *Life of Anne Radcliffe*.

There was evidently a certain tension within that poor old head, which suddenly eased. Miss Jebb's teeth became visible, the set still complete although they were yellow and strangely elongated. At the same time, a loud dry laugh sounded out of nowhere, and the voice of Miss Jebb–which emerged, this time, from under the table–said: "Very well, very well! Since the gentleman has come a long way and is Your Ladyship's guest, he shouldn't go away with nothing to show for his journey. I still hope that you will able to call me Miss Hundred one day, but I have been suffering from autumnal headaches for the first time in my life, and I don't want to carry this incredible story to the grave."

No sooner had she said it than we were all ears. Miss Jebb set down her cup and seemed to gather herself together. During the silence which followed, she shuddered briefly on two or three occasions, producing a sound like hazelnuts rattling in a paper bag.

"There has never been another tale like it," she murmured, at last, clasping her hands about her knees to prevent them from shaking. "I grow cold when I think of it, in the very depths of my heart. I don't know whether I ought to break my silence, but what can it matter? I should like Her name to be on everyone's lips one last time–and they will certainly talk, for it is terrible... terrible!"

One

Miss Anna spent her early childhood in the house where her parents, Mr. and Mrs. Ward, conducted their business. They were not rich, but they had very good connections. When Mr. Ward sold his establishment, in 1776 or thereabouts, he brought his wife and daughter to live in the cottage in which we are now gathered [5].

Anna's adolescence flowed peacefully and happily by in this retreat, where "the mediocrity of gold"–as the poet has it–reigned supreme, sustaining that modest ease which is called good fortune.

During holidays especially, the cottage came to life. Then we would entertain Cornelia de Witt [6] with her governess, Signora Letizia, and a blithe young man named Edward S. Barton, accompanied by his tutor Otto Goetzi.

Anna, Edward and Cornelia were bound together by a firm friendship. It was virtually taken for granted that Ned Barton would marry Anna when he came of age. I remember that Mrs. Ward had begun to embroider, ten years in advance, a superb pair of muslin curtains in which the monograms of Anna and Edward were interwoven–but man proposes and God disposes. It transpired that Ned Barton and our Anna loved one another only as brother and sister. I am sure that was true of Ned; perhaps there was a little something more in the dear heart of Anna, but William Radcliffe was nevertheless the happiest of husbands–Sir Walter Scott says so in his account of her life [7].

The world being as it is, there can never have been such natural grace as Anna's. And what exuberance! Wherever she went, the room filled with smiles. Her only fault was an excessive timidity. Never judge authors by their works! It is not a hundred but a thousand times that I have been asked where she found the melancholy inspiration of her genius. You, at least, when you have heard me out, will never ask me that question again.

The month of September 1787 saw the last holiday shared by our three friends. William Radcliffe had already added a fourth to their number. He had asked for the hand of Miss Ward in July of that same year. Ned and Cornelia had been engaged during the previous winter; they were very much in love with one another and the life that was in prospect for them seemed to hold every promise of success.

On this occasion, Monsieur Goetzi did not accompany his maturing pupil, who was already sporting–honourably, of course–the uniform of the Royal Navy. For her part, Letizia had stayed in Holland, where she was serving as housekeeper to Count Tiberio, Cornelia's tutor. To illustrate how beautiful Cornelia was, one must have recourse to the eloquence of my poor Anna, who was later to immortalize the charms of her friend in *The Mysteries of Udolpho*–Cornelia was the original on whom the character of Emily is based.

Oh, the memories! I was still a child, but I remember our long walks in the hills. Mr. Radcliffe had hardly a trace of romanesque precision; he was proper, well-dressed and polite to the fairer sex. Every time Ned and Cornelia lost themselves in the woods, William Radcliffe tried to strike up a conversation with Anna that was pleasant and tender, but she would immediately call out to me and turn the discussion towards literary topics. At her request, Mr. Radcliffe would recite passages from Greek and Latin poets. Although she could hardly understand their meaning, *She* was in love with their learned music–and sometimes, while the graduate of Oxford was declaiming Homer or Virgil, the soft gaze of our Anna would lose itself in the distance, where Midshipman Ned and the pale Cornelia were wandering, as if in a dream...

She would sigh then, and request Mr. Radcliffe to translate the text, word by word–which he did with a good grace, always happy to oblige [8].

The farewells were sad, that year. They all knew that they would not see one another again until both marriages had taken place: that of Mr. Radcliffe and Anna at this very place, and that of Ned and Cornelia in Rotterdam, where Count Tiberio made his home.

In response to a delicate and sentimental impulse, they had arranged that both marriages would take place on the same day, at the same hour: one in Holland; the other in England. By that means, in spite of the distance between them, a kind of communion would be established between the two happy events.

From the end of the vacation to the time of the double marriage, a very active correspondence was maintained. Cornelia's letters were filled with the purest joy. As for Ned, he was as amorous as a whole battalion of lovers. I did not see our Anna's replies, but she seemed to me to be a little sad.

At Christmas, the plans for the wedding were set in motion. Throughout the month of January 1787, there was no other matter of discussion but the *trousseau*. The great day had been fixed for the third of March.

In February, a letter arrived from Holland which threw the household into turmoil. The dowager Countess of Montefalcone, *née* de Witt, had died in Dalmatia. Cornelia, her sole heiress, suddenly found herself in possession of an enormous fortune.

The letter was from Ned, who seemed disturbed and rather saddened by this occurrence.

Although the missive was very short, it found space to record the singular fact that Count Tiberio, by virtue of the bountiful inheritance of the dowager of Montefalcone, now found himself the immediate heir of his own pupil.

After this letter, no further news was received from Holland until the end of February. There was nothing particularly surprising in that: bad weather held sway over the Channel and the wind, which blew incessantly from the west, made the crossing difficult. Today's steampackets make a mockery of the stiffest wind but in those days weeks could pass without any word arriving from the continent.

Every morning, as was his habit, the excellent Mr. Ward would look up at the weathervane atop the cottage and say: "As soon as that cock turns around, we'll get a whole ream of letters all at once!"

The first two days of March also passed without news. The wedding was to take place the following day; the house was full of activity and noise.

An hour after dinner, as evening approached, the wedding-gown was delivered–and almost at the same instant, the bell at the gate rang. The joyous voice of Mr. Ward was heard proclaiming from the staircase: "I said as much the day before yesterday: the cock has turned around! Here's the postman, bearing a whole armful of letters!"

Truth to tell, the arrival of the letters was rather inconvenient, given that the house was in such turmoil. The packet's contents were abundant and the dates of the postmarks very various. There was only time to open the most recent, in order to ascertain that our friends in Rotterdam were well, before everyone went back to work.

Under pressure of time, Anna was the prisoner of the couturiers who had brought her dress. I carried a batch of envelopes up to her myself, consisting of five letters–three from Cornelia and two from Ned Barton. At her request, I opened the one which seemed to be the latest, and went immediately to the foot of the fourth page.

"All is well," I said, after having scanned several lines.

"God be praised!" cried our Anna.

"Now, my angel," exclaimed the dressmaker, "little Jebb must show us a clean pair of heels–you're getting in our way, dear treasure."

She smiled at me to ameliorate the harshness of the instruction that chased me away. She was like a martyr assailed by four harpies with mouths full of pins, who were securing her within her shrine of white muslin. I put the packet of letters on the side-table and I left.

I should call your attention at this point to an important item: it is at this precise moment that I cease to speak as an actual eye-witness. From now on, it is to Anne Radcliffe herself that you are listening, for it was from her own lips that I had the rest of the story. I only saw her again after the events had taken place.

It was about seven o'clock in the evening when the dressmaker and her assistants left the house, carrying the wedding-gown away one last time in order to make the final alterations

When she was left alone, our Anna felt so utterly exhausted by the commotion of the day that she lacked the strength to come down to the parlor where her father, mother and fiancé were waiting. She offered herself the excuse that she had to give proper attention to the letters from Rotterdam, but sleep claimed her before she had reached the end of the first paragraph of a joyous letter bearing the signature Edward S. Barton.

Our Anna's sleep was feverish and filled with dreams. She saw a little church, framed in an unusual style, set in a pleasant countryside filled with trees and plants that did not grow in England. There were blankets of corn in the fields and the cattle had hides colored like turtle-doves. Beside the church was a cemetery whose tombs were all white. There were two among them that seemed to be identical, from each of which–a simple but touching motif one often encounters in English cemeteries–*an arm extended, sculpted in a substance whiter than marble*. The two arms stretched towards one another, so that their hands clasped.

She did not understand, in her dream, why the sight of those two sepulchres made her shiver and weep bitterly. *She* wanted to read the inscriptions engraved on the marble headstones, but it was impossible to do that. The letters became jumbled and fled before her gaze.

At ten o'clock, when the noise of the returning dressmakers woke her up, *She* was still in tears. *She* had slept for three hours but the weight of a terrible unhappiness lay upon her mind.

"I shall not ask why you have such red eyes, Miss Ward," the dressmaker said to her. "Young girls about to be married always weep, and I suppose they are entitled. Try the dress on."

The dress was tried on. It fitted well, and they left her alone again. *She* bathed her eyes. The couturier's words had brought back the impression of her dream. Her gaze happened to fall upon the letters from Rotterdam which she had almost forgotten, and a loud gasp escaped her bosom.

It was as if she could suddenly read the names inscribed on the marble of the two identical tombs: Cornelia! Edward!

She opened an envelope at random. Her over-anxious eyes saw nothing at first but black dots dancing on the white sheet. When she was finally able to read, she was quickly reassured. The letter had been written on the thirteenth of February by Cornelia, who was happily making plans for the next holiday. By that time, the will of the dowager countess would have been sorted out. Cornelia intended to come to the cottage, not to stay there as she normally did but to collect the whole family and convey them to Castle Montefalcone, in the Dinaric Alps beyond Ragusa [9]. She had a huge estate there, with marble and alabaster quarries. She was beside herself with joy. Ned had fallen in love with a poor girl, but now she was suddenly able to make him a rich landowner...

"What would I have given him?" our Anna thought, as she folded the letter. "It is better this way–and William is a worthy soul, after all."

Because she had already slept for three hours, she no longer felt tired. She settled down in a comfortable armchair and resolved to read the rest of her correspondence through to the end.

The happiness of her dear Cornelia delighted her, and you will understand that although a few sighs disturbed the muslin of her bodice, they were not provoked by envy. Anna envious–what blasphemy! No, but it is certainly true that Corny dwelt a little too much upon her new riches, her finery–and, above all, on the ardor of the attentions lavished upon her by the enraptured Ned. Entire pages sang like psalms, and vaulting over the psalms of Miss Corny came the dithyrambs of Edward Barton. Joy! Love! Love! Joy! It became monotonous. You have a nice saying in France: If you are rich enough, eat dinner twice! Perhaps our Anna thought: "They should be married twice, since they love one another so much."

She began to take a certain pride in comparing the moderation of her own proper affection with the delirium of Cornelia. Then, when she had become philosophical, thoroughly imbued with the kind of sagacity with which Christians regard pagans, she began to tell herself that an excess of happiness could easily be transformed into its opposite. Such is human existence: action and reaction. Whosoever wins will lose–and beyond every horizon there are clouds on their way to screen the brightest sun.

As soon as this thought was formed in our Anna's head, it established itself with a remarkable authority. It struck a chord there. She began to dread, in advance, the miseries which could so easily succeed that deluge of felicities, in the near or distant future. Dear Ned! Poor Corny! Sorrow is so cruel when it follows joy! I believe that our Anna shed a few tears after having discovered the serpent lurking beneath the roses of the voluminous correspondence–because it was there, in the letters; oh yes, it was there!

I said there were five, and that was no lie, but they were separated within like those Chinese boxes that are nested one within another, to the continuing astonishment of little children. Cornelia's letters contained Ned Barton's interjections, while his permitted hers to spring forth within, and our Anna read on and on. She was on tenterhooks. It seemed to her that she might have been reading forever–and at the very moment when the philosophical idea came to her–the idea that well-educated people render as "The Tarpeian rock is very close to the Capitol"–a corresponding change overcame the letters.

A cloud, distant as yet, appeared in the blue sky. She saw it grow, advance, darken, concealing in its skirts... but we must not get ahead of ourselves. The thunderstorm will break soon enough.

I don't know if you are like me, but every time within this incomparable story that *She* employs that formula, whose inventor she was–*we must not get ahead of ourselves*–my flesh crept.

Little by little, the correspondence of the two lovers of Rotterdam changed its character.

As chance would have it, Anna had opened the oldest letters first. The cloud rose above the horizon when she opened the earlier of the last two envelopes.

It began as a letter from Ned; the song had descended into a lower key. So far, Count Tiberio, that paragon of tutors, had never been mentioned by Ned's pen without a gesture of indulgence, kindness or generosity. This time, the not-very-august name arrived bare of any adjective. Even more disturbing, Ned had not much to say about love.

Vaguely–very vaguely–he hinted that the inheritance of the dowager countess might possibly cause trouble. Count Tiberio's demeanor had changed. Monsieur Goetzi, who was passing through Rotterdam, had insinuated peculiar things...

There followed a letter from Corny, who was evidently suffering from "nerves." She called Letizia Pallanti "that person." Yesterday's angel, that "perfect creature" Letizia! Why? It was unexplained–but between the irritated lines of the missive, our Anna's perspicacity divined one utterly shocking thing: Letizia, neglectful not merely of universal morality but even of the most common decency, had entered into a relationship with Count Tiberio which it would be superfluous to describe.

As for Monsieur Goetzi–this was a more recent letter–what part was he playing? He spoke very ill of Count Tiberio, saying that his scandalous conduct had thrown his affairs into chaos, and he passed entire mornings and afternoons locked in Count Tiberio's office! He was present at all the orgies (the very word written in the letter) and when "that creature" Letizia emerged sporting diamonds, Monsieur Goetzi would play up to her like a cavalier!

Think of the lateness of the hour! It was already long past the time when *She* had heard the chimes of midnight but she felt not the slightest need of sleep. Our Anna was consumed by a fervent desire to know what it was that had taken root in her good heart. She read on and on. A strange wedding-eve!

As the reading proceeded, the vague menace became distinct. Happiness and security induced boredom, but as the cloud gathered on the distant horizon, her interest reawakened.

As the first thunderclap sounded, *She* leapt suddenly from her armchair. A note of Ned's spoke of "delay"–and it was the marriage that was delayed!

The explanation was given by the statement that the inheritance was a splendid thing, but a little complicated, and that it was necessary to go to the place...

Why did the two not get married beforehand?

That was exactly the question that poor Ned posed.

She unfolded page after page, finding medium-sized leaves within the larger ones and smaller ones within the medium-sized. She read on and on. The most recent envelope had already been opened, when Mr. Ward had extracted from it the reassuring letter that had occasioned his cries of joy.

But do you know what that brave man had read? And I too, in my turn–for I had been similarly deceived.

We had read, here and there, two or three fragments of paragraphs in which the word "happiness" had been repeated one more time–but, alas, it was to express the regret of happiness lost!

"At the moment when all was smiles," poor Ned wrote, indeed, "when the future presented itself to us in the brightest colors: happiness, wealth, love..."

Mr. Ward had not inquired any further, and nor had I. But the sentence went on:

"...the storm burst. Yes, at that very moment; we were struck by lightning and cast down; we are lost!"

Lost! Imagine our Anna's state of mind.

Unhappily, there was no exaggeration in that fateful word! A note added by the unfortunate Cornelia read: "Torn from my bed in the middle of the night. Monsieur Goetzi seizes my hand at the foot of the stair and says: 'Courage! You have a friend!' Should I believe him? I am dragged away... The night is horrible and the tempest drowns my pleas to be sensible..."

She let go of the paper and fell to her knees.

"Oh Lord of All," she cried, between sobs, "why do you permit such heinous crimes? Where are you now, Cornelia? Where are you, my dearest friend?"

Other women usually faint in similar situations, but *She* was superior to the rest of her sex. Without abandoning her prayerful posture, she seized the letters again and continued to read through her tears. Ned seemed to respond to the last question which had sprung to our Anna's mind.

"Monsieur Goetzi had warned me," he wrote, in a few scarcely-legible lines, "but I did not want to believe him. What part is that man playing? This morning, I found Count Tiberio's house deserted. In the street the neighbors had gathered, crying: 'They have taken flight like thieves! The bankruptcy will be enormous!' 'You're wide of the mark,' replied Monsieur Goetzi, who had sprung forth as if from the ground. 'There will be no bankruptcy, and Count Tiberio will pay everyone, for he will marry the heir to the immense Montefalcone fortune!' "

One letter remained; a scrap of paper on which Ned had painfully scribbled: "Last evening, Monsieur Goetzi came to my house. He seemed to sympathize with my distress. He has told me that my beloved Cornelia, abducted by her infamous tutor, is on her way to Castle Montefalcone in Dalmatia. He advised me to hasten in pursuit. A saddled horse was ready and waiting outside my door. I set forth, although my strength was near-exhausted. No sooner was I out of town than I was surrounded and attacked by four men with their faces obscured by masks. Nevertheless, by the light of the moon and through the holes in one of the masks, I believe I recognized that green light which shines in the eyes of Monsieur Goetzi. Is it possible? A man who has been my teacher! They left me for dead on the highway. I lay there until morning, losing blood from twenty wounds. At daybreak, villagers who were carrying their produce to market took me up and carried me to a nearby inn, which bears the sign *Ale and Amity*. May God reward them! Not that I value my life, but Cornelia has no one but me to defend her. My bed is good. My room is large. It is decorated with prints displaying the battles of Admiral Ruyter. The curtains have floral designs. The innkeeper seems harmless, but he resembles Monsieur Goetzi from behind. *He has no face*, which produces a peculiar effect. He is accompanied everywhere by an enormous dog which has, by contrast, a human figure. In the wall directly in front of my bed, eight feet above the ground or thereabouts, is a round-shaped opening like those which give access to stove-pipes. In the darkness above the hole I can distinguish something green: eyes which watch me incessantly... I am, God be praised, quite composed. A doctor has been summoned from Rotterdam to look after me. He and his pipe must outweigh three Englishmen. There is a hint of green in his eyes. Do you happen to know whether Monsieur Goetzi ever had a brother...?

"A little boy five or six years old came into my room rolling a hoop. He demanded of me in an impertinent manner: 'Are you the dead man?'—and he threw a folded paper on to my coverlet. It was a letter from Cornelia... I scarcely had time to hide the paper. A bald woman came in, followed by the dog which now seems to look at me with the eyes of Monsieur Goetzi. It never barks. The innkeeper has a parrot that he carries everywhere on his shoulder and which says incessantly: 'Have you dined, Ducat?' The green eyes transfix me from the depths of the black hole. The child laughs heartily in the courtyard, crying: 'I have seen the dead man!' Around me, everything is green. Anna, my dear Anna, help...!"

Two

She got up right away, for she had not merely read the final word but *understood* it.

Within and without her mind, a double voice that sounded like the reunited voices of Cornelia de Witt and Edward Barton distinctly pronounced the words: "Help us! Help us!"

She strode back and forth across the room, in the grip of feverish distress. Then her thoughts turned again to God. *She* felt calmer.

Having been called, what could she do but go? *She* must go to their aid. How? *She* had no idea. The consciousness of her weakness was crushing, but there was something in her that was great and indomitable: her will.

She would save Edward and Cornelia.

A powerful effort calmed her fever. She was able to collect her thoughts. Who could she ask for help? Mr. Ward was old and his prudence was notorious. William Radcliffe, her intended husband, was certainly young enough, but he was a lawyer. Doubtless there are lawyers who are as brave as lions, but it is not their calling. In the end, our Anna concluded that she should not approach Mr. Radcliffe.

It was the same with the other friends gathered in the house: peaceful folk best suited to backgammon and card-games. *She* was kind enough to think of me for a moment, but I was definitely too small–and yet, it was necessary to get moving.

The first light of dawn was illuminating the curtained window. She pulled a little case into the middle of the room and threw the necessary items into it haphazardly. I do not think that she had made an actual decision to set off secretly on a long journey on the very morning of her wedding–no, she had a proper respect for convention–but there are certain things that we do without thinking, and this was one of them.

It was about four-thirty or five in the morning. Everyone in the cottage was asleep as she slipped through the corridors, carrying her case.

Grey Jack, the handyman, slept in a room on the ground floor, next door to the pantry. She knocked gently on his door and said to him: "Wake up, Jack, my friend; I have to speak to you about something important."

The good servant immediately leapt from his bed, rubbing his eyes. "What is it, Miss?" he asked. "Today, we must all begin calling you Madam! What a day! What the devil are you doing up at this hour?"

She replied: "Get dressed quickly, Jack my good friend. You are needed."

Hearing those words frightened him. When the lamp had been lit, he could see her, and was terrified. *She* was paler than a corpse. "Has something bad happened in the house?" he stammered.

"Yes," she replied, "something very bad has happened, but not in the house. Get dressed, Jack, for God's sake!"

The old man was all a-tremble, but he put on his clothes with all due haste. When he was dressed, she continued: "Grey Jack, do you remember your friend Ned Barton, whom you dandled on your knees, and Corny, the little girl from Holland?"

"Of course I remember Mr. Edward and Miss Cornelia!" the old man exclaimed. "Aren't they getting married this morning, on the other side of the sea?"

"You liked them both very much, didn't you, Jack?"

"Very much indeed–and I still do."

"Good! Jack, Johnny must be harnessed to the cart and driven across country to town."

"Who by? Me?" cried the stupefied fellow. "I must leave the house on your wedding day! You'll get married without me!"

"I won't get married without you, Jack, because I'm going with you." He would certainly have protested, but she added: "It's a matter of life and death!"

Grey Jack, totally bewildered, ran to the stable without asking for any further explanation. Reluctantly, he did as he was told. From time to time, he looked back at the windows to see if anyone else had got up–but everyone was still in bed. The whole world was asleep.

She took her place in the cart.

Grey Jack climbed up on to the driver's seat. Johnny broke into a trot.

No one in the house awoke. *She* felt a constriction in her heart. Although she had not yet composed any of her admirable works, she already possessed the brilliant and noble style which Sir Walter Scott was to praise to the skies in his biography. Indeed, she could not help exclaiming: "Goodbye, dear refuge. Happy shelter of my adolescence, adieu! Verdant countryside, proud hills, woodlands full of trees and mystery, shall I ever see you again?"

Grey Jack, who was not in a good mood, turned to her and said: "Instead of talking to yourself, Miss, you would do better to tell me why we are going to Stafford so early."

"Grey Jack," she said, solemnly, "we are not bound for Stafford."

Grey Jack turned to her, open-mouthed. "Miss," he said, while his huge eyebrows drew together, "for twenty-three years you have been whiter than a lamb, but if you are using me to run away from your father and mother's house, I'll be damned..."

She cut him off with a gesture, and said: "Don't jump to any conclusions, Jack. Just go–to Lichfield! [10]"

Even the most beautiful girl in the world could only give what she had. I am recounting the tale to you as she told it to me. *She* did not bother to fill in certain details. For instance, no exact account of the cycle of day and night figured in her narrative. *She* passed over such mere trifles, carried onwards by memories that soared like the winged horse Pegasus, symbol of the imagination of poets.

You are entitled to suppose that *She* ate meals, for her stomach was of the same superior quality as the rest of her being. She slept too, equally well, but these diverse functions and all those which debase our nature we shall pass over in silence.

Another matter on which subject our Anna always disdained to furnish me with any details was the question of money. In that respect, Milady and Monsieur, you may formulate your own hypotheses with all the ingenuity of which you are capable. The journey was long and confounded by the most extraordinary obstacles. She was continually required to open her purse. Whence did she draw those expenses? I don't know, and wash my hands of the matter. The fact is that she paid her way and returned to the fold without having left a single outstanding debt.

Between Stafford and Lichfield, Grey Jack, who had had a good meal, became more inquisitive.

"I suppose, Miss, that Miss Corny and that strapping lad Ned are waiting for you down there with a third gallant? Am I right? William Radcliffe doesn't know about this, does he? It doesn't matter–here in England there's no shortage of vicars to marry two young people at the drop of a hat. But who would have thought it of you, Miss Anna? Not me."

Instead of replying, *She* asked: "What do you think of Otto Goetzi, Jack?"

The old man nearly fell off his seat with astonishment. "What! Miss! Is it for that scruffy devil that you have scorned such a gentleman? Master William is certainly a queer bird, but..."

"I beg you to speak more respectfully of my husband, Jack!"

"Your husband! Now I don't understand anything at all!"

"I asked you what you thought of Monsieur Goetzi."

"I think that I would like to be in Lichfield in order to get to the bottom of this," replied the old man, in a bad humor. "As for Mr. Goetzi, he's not the first scoundrel I've seen well-supported and well-nourished by good families while pretending to teach young children."

The horse shied. Grey Jack crossed himself. "See what happens when his name is spoken aloud," he muttered. "No one knows anything about the man, except that he is a vampire."

"I don't believe in vampires, my friend," said our Anna, disdainfully. *She* was above belief in the superstitions that flourished in the hills between the counties of Staffordshire and Shropshire [11].

"Is that so?" replied the old man. "One has to believe in vampires. They come from the Turkish lands, a long way off, beyond the city of Belgrade. Only, I don't know exactly what they are. There's nothing you don't know—would you like to explain it to me, Miss?"

Like all educated people, *She* loved to instruct others. "Vampires," she said, "supposing that they exist, are monsters in human form, who originate from southern Hungary, between the Danube and the Sava. Their nourishment is the blood of young women..."

"That's right, Miss," cried Grey Jack, impetuously. "I have seen him with my own eyes!"

"Monsieur Goetzi—drinking the blood of a young woman?" said Anna, horrified.

"For want of a better word. It was Jewel, Miss Corny's little spaniel. What a darling! Do you remember? He stalked and drank the blood of the little creature, like the disgusting weasel he is. And he stole raw cutlets from the kitchen! And he got up at night to talk to spiders! And everyone knows that was how Polly Bird of the High Farm died—found asleep by the side of the stream and never woke up. And whenever he goes into a room all the lamps glow green. Can you deny or disprove it? And what of the tomcats which leap upon his back because he stinks worse than a she-cat in heat? And you ought to understand what the washerwoman says about him: all his shirts have a faded bloodstain in the place next to his heart!"

"My friend," she said to him, "those are the sort of rumors which circulate among common folk. I need something more definite. Don't you know why Monsieur Goetzi was dismissed from the house of Squire Barton?"

"Of course! Any child would be able to tell you that. It was because of Miss Corny. Squire Barton valued Mr. Goetzi highly as a man of learning, and he was like you–he didn't believe in vampires. It was because Miss Cornelia contracted a chest complaint and began *to see green*, and... that's odd, Miss Anna–look at the moon!"

The near-full moon had risen behind a screen of leafless poplars. Our Anna had the courage of a hero, but she could not help shuddering when she saw that *the moon was green*.

"Go on, I beg you," she murmured.

"That's what happens," Grey Jack murmured, "when one talks about him. One morning Miss Cornelia was found unconscious in her bed. Upon her left breast there was a little black puncture-wound, and Fancy, your chambermaid, saw a green spider of unusual size disappearing under the door. She followed it. The spider ran so swiftly along the corridor that Fancy couldn't catch up, but she perceived that it went into Mr. Goetzi's room. She found Ned Barton, the dear boy–who did not much like his tutor, it's true. Ned went into Mr. Goetzi's room and beat him so vigorously..."

"The wretch!" Anna put in, bringing her hands together. "Is this true? Did Ned really thrash that pernicious and vindictive creature?"

"With his fists, yes Miss, and kicked him too, and hit him with a cane and a chair. And Mr. Goetzi went to complain to the squire, who gave him a sum of money..."

They arrived in London that evening. *She* went, with Grey Jack, to see the Olympic Circus in Southwark. *She* was in no mood for frivolity, but there was no boat due to leave before the following morning and the idea

47

of going to the circus was suggested to her by a peculiar coincidence.

One particular word leapt out at her from the extraordinary profusion of posters advertising the event: the word *VAMPIRE*.

Between the bills which advertised the clever horse that could walk on its hind legs, and the ones promoting the clown Bod-Big, who could swallow a mole and regurgitate it alive, there was inscribed in green letters:

MAIN ATTRACTION!!!
THE DEVOURING OF A YOUNG VIRGIN
BY THE AUTHENTIC VAMPIRE OF PETERWARDEIN
WHO WILL DRINK SEVERAL PINTS OF BLOOD
AS IS HIS HABIT
WITH THE MUSIC OF THE HORSEGUARDS
WONDERFUL ATTRACTION INDEED!!!

When *She* and Jack went in together, the immense circus-tent was full of spectators. They were watching an old woman painted with gilt, standing upright on a galloping horse. She leapt through paper circles, to the immense delight of the huge crowd. It was the famous Lily Cow.

Afterwards, the candles were extinguished–the age of gaslight had not yet arrived–and darkness fell, to be succeeded by a phosphorescent glow which reflected lividly from the faces of the spectators all around the amphitheater. Lightning flashed in the distance, and a pervasive moaning wind was heard. The music became grating.

An enormous spider, which had the body of a man and the wings of a vulture, was lowered down on a thread which hung down from above, stretched by its weight.

At the same time, a young Czech girl, hardly more than a child, dressed in white and mounted on a black horse, entered the ring. Balanced on her head was a garland of roses. She was sweet and beautiful, that young girl. She bore a slight resemblance to Cornelia de Witt, and–strangely enough–the resemblance grew the more clearly she was seen.

The spider curled itself up at the bottom of its thread; it no longer moved, but lay in wait. While it was thus immobilized, a distinct aura of green radiance could be seen surrounding it, most intensely at the center, weakening towards the periphery.

The young Czech played with her flowers and danced.

All of a sudden, the spider let itself fall from its thread. Its long and hideous legs flowed over the sand that carpeted the ring. The young girl saw it and made her fear manifest by means of diverse mimetic poses, which won her abundant applause.

The spider pursued the young girl, who fled as fast as she could to her black steed. The monster went after her, with uncertain strides. Unable to gain sufficient purchase on the surface, it adopted an expedient typical of its kind. I do not know exactly how to describe the manner in which it took her, but it carried filaments hither and yon, which appeared to emerge from its mouth. Within the blink of an eye, it had spun a web: a spider-web!

The young girl was on her knees on the back of her horse. She threw away her garland, threw away her veils; clad only in flesh-colored tights she made a touching sight. Suddenly, the spider trapped her in its web. It was horrible. The horse, still free, darted right and left.

There was a sound of grinding bones.

It was not a spider, but actually a man who was seen to drink deep draughts of red blood through a blaze of green light.

The circus-tent shook with the volume of the applause, but Anna fell into a faint, crying: "Monsieur Goetzi! It is Monsieur Goetzi! I recognized him!"

There is no country in the world where the principle of liberty is so splendidly applied as in England. Nevertheless, I do not think that our laws permit the exhibition on the public stage of an authentic vampire crunching the bones and drinking the blood of a real girl. That would be too much.

I believe therefore that you can take it for granted that the administrators of the Southwark Circus produced the illusion by the means that they were accustomed to employ. The proof of this is that the young horsewoman, devoured by the vampire, was pulverized and drained in like manner every night for several weeks, and was none the worse for it.

As regards the question of knowing whether the monster was really Monsieur Goetzi, I do not believe it, although we are assured that these exceptional creatures called vampires or accursed wanderers have the gift of ubiquity—or at least of *alibi-ty*, if I may be permitted to invent the word.

Our Anna's error can be explained by virtue of one of those resemblances which are so common in nature. The majority of authors agree that all vampires exhibit a family resemblance, as if they were the sons or nephews of the same stallion sire.

It would be very foolish to suppose, no matter what was described just now, that Monsieur Goetzi could have taken the trouble to abandon the important matters which required his attention in Holland in order to perform as an acrobat.

Three

The crossing was uneventful. Grey Jack ate and slept. *She*, on the other hand, propped herself up against the bulwark in one of those correct and noble poses which she naturally assumed, watching the frothy wake churned up by the vessel's passage. Her eyes were trying to penetrate the immense profundity of the sea. The waves were suggestive of infinity.

Once they had passed out of the Thames estuary Grey Jack woke up, saw the land on the horizon, and asked for a drink. *She* made him sit down beside her and recounted with marvelous exactitude the incoherent ravings that she had read on the eve of her wedding.

"Such is the sum," she reported, "of that unhappy correspondence. It turns out that Count Tiberio, the tutor of my cousin Cornelia, is a *débauché*, and also that his business is in a perilous state. As for Letizia Pallanti–a well-born person does not deign to mention creatures of that sort. The two of them have seized Cornelia and have taken her to the mountains of ancient Illyria. Do you think that such force could have any honorable intention? The infamous Tiberio is my cousin's heir. O Heaven! I dare not think of what might happen to my dear Cornelia in the wilderness of Dalmatia, which civilization has been so slow to penetrate."

"The fact is," said Grey Jack, "that the more one thinks about it, the more content one is to be in England. But who will sow the spring seeds if you take me off chasing all the devils in Hell? Will you have the goodness to tell me that?"

"While you are asking me frivolous questions, Edward Barton, stabbed by four hired bandits, has been delivered into the care of mercenaries. His last letter did not even mention Merry Bones..."

"That Irish rogue!" Grey Jack exclaimed, with sudden violence.

"The Irish are Christians, like us, my friend," Anna pointed out, gently. Try telling that to a man who is English to the core! Jack's fists had clenched at the mere mention of Merry Bones, who was Edward Barton's valet.

This Merry Bones, Old Jack's enemy, bore some resemblance to a bundle of firewood. His figure was defined by very big bones, which had hardly any flesh upon them, and when he laughed, his mouth split his face from ear to ear. A merry companion indeed! His right eye was huge and his left so tiny that it seemed to be the child of the other. His hair was so coarse that it was impossible for him to wear a hat; he plaited it like the tail of an American horse. He had once been a mariner, but he had spent the greater part of his career as a "nailhead" in a public house in Whitefriars.

A "nailhead" is the name given to those Irishmen who hire out their skulls for sixpence to test the fists and canes of gentlemen. They charge a whole shilling for a cudgel. If asked, Merry Bones would go as far as to take a saber-thrust for half a crown.

The boat put in at Ostend and then set out again for Rotterdam. Moving along the coast of that unique and celebrated territory, Anna could not help but think of the great historic events which bound England's past to Holland's; but as the vessel progressed northwards by degrees, passing the mouths of the channels one by one, the importance of the matter in hand reasserted itself.

Night was falling when the boat entered the estuary of the Meuse; by the time they reached the port of Rotterdam the darkness was complete. Innkeepers were eager to attract their custom, but they were not so tired as they had been the day before; in reply to the various solicitations, Anna said: "I don't want to stay at any inn in town, but can anyone tell me the location of a country hostelry known by the name of *Ale and Amity*?"

The men gathered by the quayside suddenly fell silent. Then one voice said: "Young lady, this is not a good time to go to a place like that!" And as if all their tongues had been loosened at the same time, a great murmur began in which only the following words could be distinguished: "Why choose the very inn where the Englishman has been stabbed?"

Although the talk was of murdered men, the Flemish tableau was not at all unpleasant. There were a dozen honest faces there, lighted as if in a Rembrandt painting by the lanterns of the hotel touts. *She* came down into the middle of the crowd, draped in her cloak and supported by the arms of Grey Jack. A few yards away flowed the Meuse, where galiots swayed heavily on the waves.

She repeated, coldly: "Does anyone know the way to this sinister place called *Ale and Amity*?"

The silence which followed these firm words was disturbed by the noise of dry derisive laughter.

"What's that?" our Anna demanded, losing none of her intrepid serenity.

Before replying, they crossed themselves.

"The wind laughs like that, ever since the Englishman was stabbed..."

"In God's name, young stranger, don't go out on the Gueldre causeway tonight, or you'll be sorry."

"Yesterday's high tide has broken the dikes."

"The road has crumbled away in more than ten places."

"It's impassable to carriages and horses alike."

"Do you hear, Miss?" Jack exclaimed. "Neither carriages nor horses! See!"

"I will go by water," said our Anna.

"The high tide has flooded the canal. No boats can enter it."

"Then I'll go on foot," she said. "There is no obstacle large enough to keep me from the road I want to take. If one among you will consent to guide me to the inn of *Ale and Amity*, I will pay the asking price–whatever it might be."

The crowd remained silent, and a distant echo could be heard of that laughter which had previously pierced the night.

At the same time, a peasant dressed in *trews* and a doublet of white linen suddenly appeared in the lighted area, pushing through the crowd. He was wearing a big Flemish hat, which was tilted over his eyes. The light of the lanterns tried to slide under the capacious rim, but nothing could be seen of his features: nothing at all. And–how can I put this?–that nothing induced a shiver.

"Who is that?" asked a chorus of low voices.

No one replied.

The peasant passed through the crowd and came to take the suitcase from Grey Jack's hands. The servant's teeth were chattering.

"The matter is settled," the newcomer said, with a voice that our Anna herself was never able to describe. "I will take you where you want to go. Follow me." And he set forth, as stiff as a man of stone but making swift headway.

She followed him, in spite of Grey Jack's supplications.

The shore was enveloped by the darkness of night, but in the distance a pale radiance could be seen, within which the group composed of the peasant, our Anna and old Jack moved with great rapidity.

It seemed that the radiance came from the peasant: it was green. The representatives of the various inns felt their flesh creep as they dispersed like a flock of ducks.

The travelers maintained a straight course, clearing the canals and fences whether or not there were bridges. It all seemed perfectly straightforward to our Anna, who went where her guide went–and Grey Jack followed in his turn. The town was behind them in the blink of an eye.

They left the town on the east side. Crossing a terrain where land and water alternated and mingled in extraordinary confusion, the journey proceeded with scarcely any difficulty. There was certainly no shortage of obstacles: the ever-present canals, rivers and marine inlets were like tangled hair, but there was an excellent system of bridges which allowed them to keep their feet dry.

After some minutes, the scene changed. I beg you to do your utmost to imagine three individuals enshrouded in near-blackness, making their way by the muted light of the stars. A dense mist was gathering, hiding both the earth and the sky.

Within this mist the peasant *shone* faintly as if his body had been rubbed with phosphorus. He had not said a word since they had set out, but he went on and on. His Flemish hat was no longer on his head. The wind stirred and twisted his hair, drawing sparks therefrom.

Then, all of a sudden, the night became clear. The entire panoply of the stars was suspended in the sky. The road ran straight and level as far as the eye could see between two meadowlands flecked with puddles like polished mirrors.

How was it that the sound of a bell could extend into that place where there was neither bell-tower nor parish church? The twelve strokes of midnight could be distinctly heard. At the twelfth, the illumination of the peasant's hair was extinguished, and the air was filled with derisive laughter.

"Help!" lamented Grey Jack.

The earth suddenly opened up to engulf them, thus confirming the presentments of our Anna.

If you balk at believing in the instantaneous formation of a deep pit, I will freely confess that the personal opinion of our Anna was that a cave-in had already taken place, caused by the high tides of the new moon. The principal charm of a narrative like ours is its realism. And besides, in making further progress we shall encounter more than enough hyperphysical incidents.

She was fond of that word–which could, I suppose, be rendered "supernatural" [12].

The pit was as black as the ink at the bottom of a well, and lined with suffocating and acridly odorous marine mud. A dark silhouette was outlined above them, gesturing in cruel triumph, and the suitcase was dropped into the abyss, displacing torrents of mud as it fell.

Grey Jack–who was, after all, only a man of common extraction–seized the opportunity to address bitter reproaches to his young mistress. "See what a pretty pickle we're in now, Miss! You should have followed the good advice I gave you. I was certain that this rascally peasant was none other than Mr. Goetzi himself, or at least one of his kin. Now, we'll perish in this cesspit!"

In the deep silence of the night, the cackle of demoniacal laughter was heard yet again, but so distantly that it was scarcely distinguishable.

Fortunately, at almost the same instant, sounds of a very different kind made themselves heard. Soft musical notes of a rustic quality became audible, mingled with bursts of cheerful laughter. At first, our Anna could not believe her ears, and Grey Jack thought that he was in the grip of the hallucinations which precede death.

Soon enough, though, it was impossible to doubt it. The sound of horses' hooves and cartwheels was approaching rapidly. The darkness, meanwhile, was relieved by brightening lights.

Eventually, at the edge of the pit opposite to that which had given way under the feet of our Anna and old Jack, a very agreeable sight presented itself. Firstly, there were young Dutch girls crowned with flowers and dressed for a holiday, whose smiling beauty was lit by the glare of many torches; a near-equal quantity of young boys followed in their train. Then came a respectable man in clerical costume–not the robes of a Catholic priest, but the dignified and austere habit of an Anglican priest. Then, last of all, came a young nobleman, a member of the finest aristocracy in all the world, no less: the English nobility.

This unknown person, fair of hair and pale of skin, with rosy-cheeks and sky-blue eyes, was positively comparable to a god.

She did not know the honorable Arthur *** from Adam, or Eve. She was certain, all the same, that she immediately *recognized* in him, firstly an Englishman, because the English "leap to the eyes" wherever one has the good fortune to run across them, just as Venus reveals her divine nature in every step she takes; secondly, one of the gentle folk, because every species of flower has its distinctive perfume; and finally, the son of a titled family, because none but the blind is denied the pleasure of classifying a star by its rays.

He was traveling incognito, perfecting his military education with a study of the historic battlefields of Germany and the Low Countries.

The young village girls crowned with flowers and clad in their Sunday best were contemplating the precipice in a somewhat crestfallen manner, saying to one another: "Look at that! We'll be late for the wedding!"

The clergyman, calm and serene, took up a position behind his pupil. "All well and good," he said, peering down into the pit. "Everything in life must be turned to profit. Tomorrow morning, I shall set you the problem of designing a bridge that would allow an army to cross this lagoon: thirteen thousand foot-soldiers, eight thousand horses and seventy-two artillery pieces of various caliber, with supply-trucks, ambulances and so on."

Immediately, the young unknown comparable to a god leaned over the pit, and lowered a torch so that he might see into it.

Our Anna could have contemplated that arresting spectacle for a lifetime, but Grey Jack–who was made of coarser stuff–had been knee-deep in mud for far too long.

"Oi!" he cried. "Are you going to leave us here, in the devil's name?"

There was sudden consternation among the villagers. The clergyman and our Anna, seized by the same thought, spoke in unison: "There's no need to such language!" Then the clergyman added: "Very well, My

Lord, consider this question very carefully: given the situation that an unknown number of persons find themselves in trouble down below–by virtue of an accident, I suppose–what mechanical means would you employ to hoist them up to firm ground, if you had a rope but lacked a pulley?"

"I would take my purse," said the adolescent, matching speech with gesture, "and I would say to these brave people here: I will give ten French silver *pistoles* if you can bring that old man and that young woman here to me, safe and sound."

I do not know whether that response would be marked correct in the military examination at Eton, but the male wedding guests needed no further encouragement. In the blink of an eye, they leapt down from the lip of the landslide, and the two friends were carried up to the roadway.

She was then able to see the magnificently-equipped coach which had accommodated the young nobleman and his estimable instructor thus far along the road, having come from Nijmegen bound for Rotterdam.

The wedding-guests, interrupted as she had been by the landslide, undertook to find another way across–but because it was necessary to retrace their route, the young unknown comparable to a god gallantly bade our Anna to climb up into the carriage, and delivered her to the very door of the inn that was known by the singular name of *Ale and Amity*.

Four

The inn was a huge building framed by pilings, situated at the intersection of four roads. It was entirely black in color. There was no hedge around it, nor any trees nearby; it gave the impression of being lost in the middle of a desert. Above the door, the guttering light of a signal-lantern flickered in the night wind.

She felt her heart constrict as she lifted the door-knocker, thinking: "Between these walls, far from his homeland, my childhood friend Edward Barton has breathed his last!"

I have nothing to report of Grey Jack, whose mud-stains extended as far as his armpits, but that he shook with fear and was in an exceedingly bad mood.

Although there seemed to be no light within the inn, the door opened at the first knock. Our Anna and Grey Jack found themselves in a low-ceilinged room which reeked of pipe-smoke.

There was a long table, furnished with benches. Empty pitchers stood upon it, their bases set in pools of spilled ale. There was a three-foot high counter defended like a fortress, on which stood a clock in a fawn-colored cabinet encrusted with gilt, surmounted by the figure of a scrawny bird.

The hands of the clock stood at one hour, less two minutes, after midnight.

All this was apparent, even though no light burned in any of the candle-brackets and it was impossible to imagine that any ray of moonlight could have crept through the closed doors and windows. It seemed at the time that the objects emitted a dull and limpid light of their own, softened with a hint of green.

61

Unmoving beneath the clock, a group of people was gathered around a big man who seemed to possess only the outlines of a face: a frame of hair and beard. He had a long-tailed parrot perched on his shoulder. To his right there was a small boy of mischievous appearance, propped up on a hoop; to his left a monstrous flesh-colored dog whose form seemed nearly human, rigidly set on its four widespread paws.

Behind the counter, a bald and extremely fat woman was asleep, snoring loudly. Apart from the ticking of the clock–which was peculiarly profound–this was the only sound that could be heard within the inn.

She experienced an indefinable sensation, which was not quite fear. She had the strangest feeling, in consequence of this ominous emotion, that the people before her were mere accessories of the pendulum: parts of a mechanical system, like the figures mounted on the Strasbourg Clock.

"If you please," Grey Jack piped up, "we would like a fire by which to dry ourselves, bread, meat and ale!"

She bade him be silent with an abrupt gesture, although his requests were perfectly reasonable, and said in her turn: "We demand to be taken immediately to Edward S. Barton, esquire–an English subject, who is or was lodged in this public house–if he is still alive. If, unhappily, he is deceased, whether by natural causes or violence–which the forces of justice will ascertain–we shall claim his corpse so that we can ensure that it receives a Christian burial."

The inhabitants of the inn made no more response to these words than they had to Grey Jack's request. All remained silent–but the silence and stillness were soon split by a voice which sounded from every part of the inn, near and distant, high and low, and which cried out in a combative Irish accent: "I'll rip out your heart and eat your soul, *begorrah*! Vile spider! Do you think that the blood of a son of Connaught can be pumped like an Englishman's? See here!"

"It's Ned's valet, Merry Bones!" *She* murmured, hope mingling with astonishment. "He must have come to his aid."

Grey Jack shrugged his shoulders and muttered: "Or the devil brought the dirty rat!"

The cries of the Irish voice continued to echo, now from the attic, now from the cellar. Our Anna–who was valor itself–was just about to run out of the ground floor room when the inner workings of the clock emitted a rumbling sound, followed by loud chiming.

It struck *thirteen times*.

As soon as it began to sound, the comatose inhabitants of the inn finally began to move. The bald woman at the counter opened her eyes; the innkeeper shifted his weight from one foot to the other; the parrot combed his master's moustache with its beak, saying "Have you dined, Ducat?" The little boy spun his hoop, crying out "I've seen the dead man", and the scrawny bird on top of the clock-case spread its enormous wings and called *cuckoo* thirteen times.

In the meantime, a door opened between the counter and the clock. A tall bony body was framed in the opening, topped by a shaggy mass of hair, like an inverted brush of the "Turk's-head" variety. Behind Merry Bones–for it was he–came a second edition, complete and exact, of the various individuals who were in the ground floor room, to wit: the innkeeper without a face, the parrot, the dog with human features, the little boy with the hoop and the fat bald woman.

The only differences were that those from without were a little paler than those within, and innkeeper number two had an enormous bludgeon in his hand.

The latter's gaze–for the place where one should have been able to see his eyes was host to a gaze–was noticeably green; and when our Anna turned her own gaze towards innkeeper number one, she saw that a bludgeon had now appeared in his hand, and that his gaze also glowed green.

A terrible battle ensued.

Merry Bones, poor devil, was caught in a crossfire. The company that was already present and the company that had just arrived flung themselves upon him all at once, with angry ferocity. The two dogs and the two children seized him by the legs, the two parrots pecked at his eyes and the two old shrews grabbed him by the neck, while the two innkeepers, alternately raising and beating down with their clubs, hammered away at his head like blacksmiths at the forge.

Paralyzed by boundless horror, *She* bore witness to that hideous assault. As for the old reprobate Jack, rendered stupid by nationalistic spite, he merely folded his arms and muttered: "It's the Irishman's problem–he can look after himself."

As it happened, the Irishman did contrive to look after himself. He was unarmed, but his head was worth as much as a cannon. Each bludgeon-blow rebounded as if from an anvil, unable even to flatten the bristly mop of his hair. I don't know how he defended his legs, his throat and his eyes, but during the entire minute that the prodigious battle lasted, our Anna did not see him receive a single wound. To the contrary, the two parrots were fluttering their wings, the two fat women were sticking out their tongues, the two little rascals were kicking their feet like overturned crabs, and the two watchdogs were held at bay, growling threateningly. As for the two innkeepers, Merry Bones butted them in the stomach one by one, and sent them sprawling against the walls in opposite directions.

It was splendid to see, even though the worthy servant had not a drop of noble blood and had first seen light of day in a despicable country.

Then he leapt over the table with a mighty bound, zoomed across the room like an arrow and disappeared through the outside door. As he went, he found the time to blow a kiss to our Anna and made a sign of a different kind to Grey Jack, whose cheeks were swollen, as if he had had three teeth extracted.

As he disappeared into the night, Merry Bones addressed himself to our Anna, saying: "See you soon! I'm off to find the iron coffin!"

If *She* had ever devoted one of her masterpieces to the subject which presently concerns us, you would find therein explanatory chapters placed at the end of the text, which would provide detailed information about the notorious but little known social class of vampires. With that possibility in mind she had made copious notes; Monsieur Goetzi–who, apart from being a member of that species, was also a man of great erudition–had furnished some useful insights.

These notes cast some light on the inhabitants of the *Ale and Amity*, human and bestial alike–for the beasts here manifest were persons as well as the people.

I shall soon have to tell you some very remarkable things about the nature of these creatures which retain certain human characteristics although they are not human. For the moment, however, I shall restrict myself to pointing out, in passing, one of the most peculiar anomalies of the vampire race: the divisibility–or, if your prefer, the *dividuality*–of such creatures. *She* employed the more scientific term.

Each vampire is a collective, represented by one principal form, but possessing other accessory forms of indeterminate number. The famous vampire of Gran, which terrorized both banks of the Danube around the town of Ofen in the 14th century, was man, woman, child, crow, horse and pike. The history of Hungary attests that Madame Brady, the vampiress of Szeged, who passed also for an oupire [13], was cockerel, soldier, lawyer and serpent.

In addition to this peculiarity, which already poses a considerable puzzle to contemporary science, it appears that each subsidiary form, like the dominant form, also has the ability to duplicate itself.

Thus, you have been able to observe that the innkeeper's family was both inside and outside the ground floor room at the same time–which made Merry Bones' situation very perilous indeed.

I shall explain one more thing, which was perhaps the strangest of all: the family of the faceless innkeeper, which you might consider, up to a point, to be a *collective* living being, could also be considered as nothing more than a mechanical system entirely composed of accessory figures, motivated as if by clockwork. The dominant form was not included among them.

You will understand everything when I add that the chief of the clan, the very soul of the group, was...yes, you have guessed! The innkeeper, his wife, his dog, his parrot, his little boy, and perhaps even the cuckoo on the clock *were all Monsieur Goetzi*! I shall provide you with convincing proof soon enough.

It is necessary that you understand that this bundle of beings, singular and plural at the same time–which seems to be the most blatant realization of the most incomprehensible mysteries of our Christian era–was not created all of a piece. It was aggregated and rounded out by conquest, like the winnings in a game of cards, or a rolling snowball. The infamous Monsieur Goetzi, having drunk the blood of all the inhabitants of the *Ale and Amity*, had incorporated them all into himself. You will readily appreciate that this facility was extremely convenient.

Five

I beg your permission, in continuing the story, to go back in time a little, in order to tell you what had already befallen those persons who are, in fact, the principal characters of this story: Edward S. Barton, Cornelia, Count Tiberio and Letizia Pallanti.

On the far side of the Rhine, to the east of the town of Utrecht and some distance from the low-lying countries which owe their existence to man's victory over the sea, the Château de Witt rose above a pleasant landscape of wooded hills. There dwelt Tiberio Palma d'Istria of the Montefalcones, who had entered into the illustrious house of de Witt by his marriage to Countess Greete, a second cousin once removed of our dear Cornelia.

Countess Greete was beautiful, well educated in letters and sciences, and as virtuous as the heavenly saints are said to be. Unfortunately, however, her education had not been extended very far in regard to the music, dance and language of Italy, which were then the height of fashion.

It was for that reason, when Cornelia's parents had died and the tutelage of the beloved infant had fallen to Count Tiberio, that she was obliged to consider appointing a governess.

Italy was then as well supplied with them as England is today. I do not know what references decided the issue in favor of Signora Pallanti, but it is certain that one could not have found another young person so accomplished had one searched the whole world. She knew almost as much as the Countess about Greek and Roman literature and had a thorough understanding of algebra and trigonometry; she could recite French tragedies, including Voltaire's, with surprising charm; she danced like Terpsichore and played the guitar, the harp, the lyre and the harpsichord; she could recite the entirety of *Jerusalem Delivered* [14] starting at the last verse and proceeding backwards to the first. (It is said that for connoisseurs, the sound of that divine poem in reverse is a delight without compare.)

Signora Letizia Pallanti might have been twenty-five years old or thereabouts. The information she gave out regarding her past was rather vague, but she was her own recommendation and her arrival at the Château de Witt was an occasion for celebration. The good Countess Greete embraced her a hundred times over.

Only Count Tiberio welcomed her, in spite of her remarkable beauty, with a cold expression. He said that he did not like women whose busts were overly endowed—Letizia was, in fact, well-equipped to give nourishment—and that prodigies intimidated him. Besides, in his opinion, the beautiful stranger did not have enough hair.

Letizia was a brunette. Her dark tresses were a trifle thin, and Count Tiberio was spoiled in that respect by the luxuriant blonde tresses of his wife, which could have been woven into a cloak had they been shorn.

Letizia, seemingly at least, was not at all put out by the attitude of Count Tiberio. She devoted herself wholeheartedly to her duties as a governess, finding abundant opportunity to return the generosity of Countess Greete, on whom she lavished every care. Cornelia, in her hands, made marvelous progress. Every evening, the whole family would come together. Greete and Letizia would sometimes enter into learned discussions of Greek or Roman poetry.

In brief, the Château de Witt presented the very image of happiness.

Cornelia adored her beautiful instructress. She brought her along on one of the journeys which she made every year to England for the holidays, and the Ward family also fell in love with the charming young woman.

I was only a child at the time, but it seems that I can see her still. Never in my entire life have I encountered a woman more seductive than Letizia.

Our Anna was equally enthusiastic–but after the events of which I speak, she told me more than once that there was an element of vague and mysterious terror mingled in the feelings she entertained towards the lovely Italian.

One thing to which I can testify myself is that Monsieur Goetzi, who was then Edward Barton's tutor, consistently manifested an extreme antipathy towards her. For her part, Letizia averted her eyes every time Monsieur Goetzi came into the room.

Even so, I caught sight of them one evening in the old chestnut-grove. Like all children, I was curious. I crept up on them. When I arrived at the place where I thought I had seen them from some way off, there was no one there. I was frightened...

Letizia departed with her pupil at the end of autumn. She had been hurriedly recalled to the Château de Witt.

Countess Greete had been counting the days until her return. Even Tiberio looked more kindly upon her, and one evening when she had been singing, the Count said: "In truth, Countess, that young person would be a marvel, were it not for her hair."

Such things are said. There is nothing unusual in it. But for some reason, Countess Greete became very pale.

It was around this time that Count Tiberio ceased to hold forth on the subject of women whose figures were a little too opulent–and while caressing the Countess Greete's hair one day, he said to her in the manner of a pleasantry: "In truth, you could share these riches with Signora Pallanti."

I am quite sure that the good Countess would not have liked anything better–but what Letizia wanted was not a part-share.

One morning, our old acquaintance Goetzi arrived at the Château de Witt, carefully keeping to himself the information that he had been dismissed from the position of tutor to Ned Barton. On the contrary, he pretended that he had come out of his way to bring Cornelia news of her kinsfolk in Staffordshire. He was politely received and he accepted the hospitality he was offered, speaking at the time of the Wards and Barton as if he still enjoyed their amity and esteem.

This was, of course, an educated man, likeable and worldly wise. In addition, he played a good game of whist, chess and backgammon. His company could have brought a new gaiety to the life of the chateau–but as things turned out, it did not. Apparently without any particular cause, Count Tiberio became thoughtful. One could not say that he drew away from his wife, but their relationship became cooler.

Countess Greete, for her part, lost a little of her equilibrium. She was uneasy; she had dizzy spells. Day by day, somehow, she was seen to grow paler, thinner–and older.

This was, I admit, by no means unusual in someone of her age, for she was no longer in her twenties. Ordinarily, though, when a beautiful woman loses her hair, it is caught by her comb and her chambermaids commiserate with her every morning regarding the ruination of her locks. In this case, there was nothing of that kind. Not a single hair remained lodged between the tortoiseshell teeth after grooming, and yet they were removed. Oh yes, they were removed!

And behold! Letizia's hair chose exactly that moment to replenish itself. One might have thought that Count Tiberio's playful wish had come true and that the beautiful Countess was sharing with Signora Pallanti.

It was not possible, of course, given that one was blonde and the other brunette; but eventually, in quantity, at least, that which Greete lost, Letizia gained.

I should point out at this point that since the arrival of Monsieur Goetzi, Letizia had been using a hair lotion recommended by the learned man—but the poor Countess tried to use it too, and found it useless. Despite the excellent restorative result obtained by the governess, Countess Greete watched despairingly as her skull shed its covering. I hesitate to write the word, but in the end it must be said: she was bald!

And she began to entertain the horrible suspicion that *la Pallanti* had somehow stolen her hair!

How could she explain it? Countess Greete did not even try. She knew only too well that the moment she broached the subject, everyone would think her mad, such was the absurdity of the idea that would be set before them. In any case, in whom could she confide? Cornelia was infatuated with her governess, and poor Greete could already hear the bursts of childlike laughter that such an extravagant claim would call forth.

Then again, how could she formulate her complaint? What proof could she offer?

There was the good Count Tiberio. of course. She could tell her beloved everything–there are no secrets between lovers–but did Tiberio still love her? Tiberio was still young and handsome; she had aged ten years in as many months. Tiberio no longer looked at her with anything but pity. He avoided her. While her lovely hair had gone to furnish the temples of Letizia, little by little, Tiberio had forgotten the way to her bedroom.

Suspicion worked its way into the Countess' head like the point of a dagger. I don't know exactly how the idea became established within her wounded spirit, but she saw Letizia as a rival to be fought and destroyed, using some part of herself as a weapon. It was, after all, her magnificent hair that Tiberio loved, even though he loved it on someone else's forehead.

The Countess was alone in her room one evening, listening to the distant sound of the harp that was being played in the drawing-room, when she was seized by an irresistible force. For the first time in many days, she went down the staircase and came to the doorway of the room where the concert was taking place. What stories the paneled walls enclosing her favorite space could have told of her former happiness!

She did not go in. Cornelia was at the harpsichord. Behind her, Tiberio and Letizia were seated on the sofa, chatting. Tiberio's fingers were bathing in the curly mass whose waves now fell upon the shore of la Pallanti's shoulders.

Countess Greete clasped both hands to the breast which housed her breaking heart. Without saying a word, she made haste to return to her room–which she was only able to attain with the aid of her old nurse Loos, whom she encountered in the corridor.

When she felt her heart beating more soundly, she said: "Listen, Loos; when I was a little girl, I told you all my troubles; today, I am so very miserable that I shall die of it."

She spoke for a long time in a weak voice, weeping all the while. Loos listened with her hands pressed together. What shocked the nurse was not the intrigue recently entered into by Count Tiberio and Letizia–the whole chateau knew about that, except for Cornelia, who was as innocent as an angel–but another circumstance reported by the unhappy Countess.

Every night, at about midnight, the Countess' insomnia was relieved for a few minutes. She fell abruptly into a heavy slumber, which was pure torture; a dream would begin–the same dream every night–in which she *sensed* that a man came into her room and quietly approached her bed, and began to pluck hairs from her head with steel pincers, tearing them out one by one. She did not know who this man was, because she was never able to open her eyes in his presence. Once he had departed, her head was gripped by a burning sensation, and the nightlight beside her bed was reflected in green from every object in the room.

That was not all. Some minutes afterwards, distant cries would break the silence: a woman's cries, which seemed to come from the wing of the house where Signora Letizia slept.

After having told this bizarre story, Countess Greete fell asleep in the arms of the old nurse, exhausted and grief-stricken.

Instead of retiring, as was her habit, the nurse slid into the space between the bed and the wall and crouched down, well hidden behind the pleats of the curtain.

Towards eleven o'clock, the harmonious sounds of the drawing-room were silenced. Some time afterwards, the Countess' breathing became louder, like that of someone who slept profoundly.

At that moment, the bedroom door opened noise-lessly, and Monsieur Goetzi appeared at the threshold. Loos could see him perfectly as he crossed the room and cautiously approached the bed. Monsieur Goetzi, be-lieving himself unobserved, allowed himself to relax entirely into his vampire self. He shone brightly green, and his lower lip burned as red as a hot iron. His hair stood on end, flowing and trembling like a flaming punch-bowl. He was a fine example of his species.

He immediately leaned over the bed. Using a long gold pin which he held between his index finger and his thumb, he pricked Countess Greete behind the left ear and promptly applied his lips to the wound. He *suckled* for ten minutes, measured out by the clock. It was be-cause of this treatment that the Countess had grown pale and aged. Her health had been cruelly affected by it–as can readily be understood, given that it was repeated every night.

Monsieur Goetzi drank, moreover, merely for nourishment, without any pleasure at all. His taste was such that none but the blood of young women could in-toxicate him. When he had taken his daily allowance, he put away the gold pin and took out a little set of pincers, by means of which he plucked hairs one by one from the Countess' head. As he took them, he arranged them in a bouquet, as if he were a gleaner arranging a sheaf of corn.

The Countess moaned feebly in her sleep. Old Loos, petrified by horror, could not believe her eyes.

As soon as Monsieur Goetzi had finished his task, he cheerfully took himself away. He was humming a song in the Serbian language, which vampires generally use between themselves.

The nurse's first impulse was to awaken the Countess, Tiberio and everybody else, and make them throw Monsieur Goetzi into a white-hot furnace. Persons of little education suppose that one can get rid of a vampire by burning him, but this is an error. However, while the old woman was stretching herself, because terror had made her limbs go numb, she heard the distant female cries of which the Countess had spoken.

She was seized by curiosity—and what difference could a few more minutes make? She emerged from her hiding-place, left the room, and moved quietly along the corridors, guided in her course by the cries.

She soon arrived at Signora Letizia's apartment, whose voice she now recognized well enough. La Pallanti wept and wailed as if she were being flayed alive. Old Loos hastily put her eye to the keyhole to see what was going on.

Through the hole, she perceived that Letizia lay upon her bed, writhing in agony. Monsieur Goetzi was standing over her with the long gold pin in his hand. You must have guessed what he was doing—and you are absolutely right. Monsieur Goetzi was making little holes with his gold pin, and he was planting the Countess' hairs in Signora Pallanti's scalp, one by one.

By now, the wrath of old Loos knew no bounds.

"Ah!" said she. "A pair of demons to be brought to account! The furnace will burn hot!"

Her anger had made her speak incautiously. Monsieur Goetzi heard her, and stopped work. That did not frighten the old woman, who set out to implement the plan that she had already worked out–but no sooner had she got up to run than she found herself face to face with Monsieur Goetzi, who barred her way. She recoiled, stupefied, saying: "How did the monster get behind me?"

Monsieur Goetzi laughed and reached out for her as she set her back against Letizia's door. The door opened behind her and the noise made her turn around again.

It was Monsieur Goetzi who came out, laughing and reaching out for her.

There were two of them! She collapsed, overwhelmed by an excess of astonishment.

Six

There were indeed two of them. That will not surprise you unduly, of course, since you are already familiar with some of the mysteries of vampiric life, but you can imagine the stupefaction of old Loos.

The Monsieur Goetzi who emerged from the room and the Monsieur Goetzi who had arrived in the corridor were so exactly alike that one would have said, seeing them come towards one another, that one man was reaching out to his image, reflected in a mirror. The gold pin was also duplicated. Each of them clutched it in his hand.

Alas, Countess Greete's unfortunate nurse had no time to marvel at the prodigy. The two gold pins touched her temples at the same time, one to the right and one to the left, and she expired without a sound.

The two monsters did not care to taste her blood; she was too old.

"My dear doctor," said one to the other, "tell me, I beg you, what we should do with the body."

"Whatever you please, my dear doctor," replied the other.

They reached out their hands, and the corpse lifted itself up on eight paws. It was a duplicate dog–two dogs, if you wish, which had the same nearly-human form. Each of them went to set itself meekly beside one of the two Doctors Goetzi, who said in unison: "He is called Fuchs. Let's get back to work." Then they embraced and blended into one, while the two dogs entered into one another.

Thus came into being the strange creature that we encountered in the inn of *Ale and Amity*.

Monsieur Goetzi returned to Letizia's bed and completed the hair-transplant.

It was during the holiday season that Countess Greete died, abandoned in a deserted house. Cornelia was here, staying with Mr. and Mrs. Ward and making the final arrangements for her marriage to Edward S. Barton. On this occasion, Cornelia was unaccompanied by her governess, Letizia having excused herself on the pretext of having family affairs to attend to in Italy.

Only much later did it become known that she had immediately followed Count Tiberio to Paris, where they proceeded to go mad, eating, drinking and gambling to extravagant excess. A belated taste for debauchery had suddenly come upon the Count, and he threw a huge party on the evening of the day when Monsieur Goetzi notified him of the death of his unhappy wife. She had died devoid of hope, with not a single thread of her magnificent hair left on her head.

The following day, Monsieur Goetzi rented a small house in the port of Utrecht, in which he installed the bald woman we subsequently discovered at the counter of the *Ale and Amity*. This woman, who obeyed him like a slave, was the remains of the Countess Greete; in Holland, where she took care of Fuchs, the dog with the human face, she was called Madame Fiole.

When the Count returned to the chateau, there was a conference between Letizia, Monsieur Goetzi and Tiberio. They discussed the recent death of the Count of Montefalcone, the richest man in the country of Istria and Dalmatia, which faces the republic of Venice on the far side of the Adriatic.

Montefalcone had left a widow and a single child. In the event of the son's death, Cornelia de Witt would

79

become the sole heir of the dowager countess–and if Cornelia were also to die, the entire Montefalcone inheritance would revert to Count Tiberio himself.

Count Tiberio was not the kind of person one would have described as a natural rogue, but he was now under the dominion of *la Pallanti*, and she was under the dominion of Monsieur Goetzi.

The conference lasted all night. It was decided there and then that Monsieur Goetzi would travel to Vienna on the business of the house–not commercial business, but bad business. It concerned the young Montefalcone, the son of the late count and the dowager countess, who was a captain in the Austrian army, attached to the Liechtenstein regiment at the court of Emperor Joseph II. He was a bad lot.

Monsieur Goetzi set out with Fiole, the bald woman, and the dog Fuchs. Our Anna did not give me details of their journey. I only know that on their arrival in Vienna they lodged at the house of a money-lender named Moses who had advanced funds to Mario Montefalcone. He held credit-notes bearing the young count's signature for more than a million florins.

He lived on the third floor of a big house in Graben with his grand-daughter Deborah, who let down a silken ladder from the balcony of her room every night for the convenience of Captain Mario.

Old Moses had a leather pocket in his overcoat, in which he always carried the notes of credit which were the cream of his fortune. He slept in his overcoat. The balcony to which the beautiful and sinful Deborah tied her silken ladder was made of iron.

One day, when there was a military parade between the hedges of the imperial castle of Schönbrunn–which were the tallest in the universe–Deborah pestered her grandfather so long and hard that he agreed to take her to see the parade. She put on her most beautiful attire and all the jewels that the captain had given her. She looked superb. Her pearls and rubies were worth exactly as much as the credit notes signed by Montefalcone, less Moses' commission. Montefalcone, for his part, had a brand new and exceedingly shiny uniform. They found one another so pleasing when the column passed by that the looks they exchanged secured the promise of a rendezvous that very night. Moses had his hand upon his leather pocket, pressing it against his heart. The whole world was happy.

But Monsieur Goetzi, Fiole and Fuchs had stayed behind to look after the house in Graben. They spent the entire time of the parade in the bedroom of the beautiful Deborah, whose blinds they had lowered. Monsieur Goetzi and Fiole worked in shifts on the balcony, with a whetstone, while Fuchs stood guard on the stair.

When Monsieur Goetzi and Diole finished work, the two upper edges of the bar that served as the balcony rail were as sharp as knives.

That night, at an hour when the square was deserted, young Count Montefalcone arrived, all wrapped up in his night-cloak and as happy as a lark. As soon as he appeared, the silken ladder fell from Deborah's balcony and the young count began to climb.

The ladder was very good, for the iron rail of the balcony, changed into a razor, took time to cut through it. It did not break until the moment when the captain had reached the second story.

There were two screams, one a woman's and one a captain's. Then the silence of the night reigned once more, like a river closing over a drowned man fallen from the parapet of a bridge.

81

At that very instant, Monsieur Goetzi woke old Moses to tell him that an evildoer was scaling the balconies of his house. The innocent went out, carrying a blunderbuss in one hand and pressing the other to his leather pocket.

Fuchs, the dog with the human form, strangled him on his own doorstep.

Monsieur Goetzi had nothing more to do in Vienna. Having emptied the leather pocket, he took to the road again, singing popular songs by moonlight with a light heart.

His escort was now further augmented. As well as the dog Fuchs and Fiole, the bald woman, he had a parrot and a little boy who played with a hoop as they went along the road. The parrot with the powerful beak and hooked talons was Moses; the urchin was the captain. This was all that had been found within the brilliant uniform.

Instead of taking the road to the Low Countries once again Monsieur Goetzi turned southwest, across the Archduchy of Austria, Carinthia and Carniola [15].

She never specified whether he traveled on foot or by carriage, but here is a rather curious detail regarding the fashion in which vampires and their accessories adopt in order to cross running water. The entire family presses against the master vampire and enter into him. When the process is complete, the master lies down on the water and sails across feet-forward like a plank. No current, however strong it might be, can grip him. Whenever you discover a person crossing a river in this feet-forward fashion, take every possible precaution, because he is most certainly a vampire.

Monsieur Goetzi veered slightly eastwards when he reached Trieste, cutting through Istria, crossing Croatia and entering Dalmatia, committing himself to the Dinaric Alps until he reached the frontier of Albania, where the Castle of Montefalcone was situated. It was one of the most imposing in the world, and had served as a stage for some of the most dramatic episodes in history.

Everything hereabouts was unruly, tumultuous and sinister, from the grass on the ground to the clouds in the sky. The mountain peaks loomed in the background with savage fervor; before them was a hurly-burly of towers, battlements and belfries, from which vast tresses of ivy fell into hundreds of ravines. Pine-trees could be seen growing in the walls, which seemed to spring up like bottomless precipices.

The overriding impression they gave was of the absolute impossibility of entering into them against the will of their master. Behind the long and narrow windows one sensed watchmen lying in ambush, deadly weapons at the ready. All the drawbridges were equipped with portcullises, hanging in the void like so many gigantic traps.

No sentinels stood upon the ramparts, but in the corner of a courtyard, lit by the horns of a moon half-immersed in a cloud as scaly and flat as a crocodile's back, there was the square frame of a gibbet, one of whose arms still bore a skeleton. Crows swirled around the other.

Monsieur Goetzi arrived some little time before sunset, pausing upon the summit of one of the highest peaks, whose face dominated the entire landscape. From there, he could see not only the castle but many towns and villages, uncultivated gorges and fertile fields, and islands in the sea. He looked long upon all these beautiful things–principally upon the domain of Montefalcone, which would indeed have suited a prince.

An indefinable smile played upon his lips, which glowed like the embers of a fire.

Suddenly he said, "Go forth!"–and his entourage of spectral slaves immediately set forth. The parrot took flight, the dog bounded down the mountain slope, followed by the bald woman and the child rolling his hoop.

Seven

When his accessories had departed, Monsieur Goetzi duplicated himself so that he would have someone to talk to. He lit a fire, and anyone who lifted his eyes that evening from the valley floor to the summit of that inaccessible peak, untrodden by any human foot, would have seen two grey shapes squatting in the snow, warmed by a livid brazier.

Night had fallen when the emissaries returned. The Castle of Montefalcone had become nothing but an undefined mass lurking amid the mountains. Here and there, behind its girdling battlements, candlelight flickered.

Although Monsieur Goetzi had said nothing to his slaves at the time of their departure, each one of them had carried out his instructions. They all returned–but at the same time, they all stayed down below, at the different posts to which they had been assigned. The faculty of duplication allowed them to render him invaluable service.

All the half-demons sat down around the fire–except for the parrot, which perched on Fiole's shoulder–and Monsieur Goetzi listened to their reports.

Fiole spoke first. "Sovereign master, I have entered the guard-house at the main gate with a barrel of kirschwasser. It seems that I have not suffered too much deterioration, because all the soldiers are trying to embrace me and call me my dear. This is what I have found out: the castle is on a war footing because of a band of brigands which infests the mountains. The garrison is strong enough to defend the town. They have one significant artillery-piece. Woe betide anyone who tries to get in that way!"

"Where is your barrel?" asked Monsieur Goetzi.

"Sovereign master," Fiole replied, "it is in the guard-room, where I am still pouring out drinks for the soldiers who call me my dear."

The dog Fuchs burst out laughing and the parrot pecked the bare head of the horrid old crone.

"Good," said Monsieur Goetzi. "Your turn, poodle."

"Sovereign lord," replied Fuchs, "I have made a tour of the fortifications. There is only one weak spot, and it will need to be further undermined if we are to go in that way. It is a gateway where there is no sentry posted, but there is a dog as big as a bull. It's lucky that we are not the same sex..."

"You've played a serenade beneath his window?" Monsieur Goetzi put in, good-humoredly.

"Yes, sovereign lord. He became fiery with passion and I have strangled him–and it is I who presently stand guard in the courtyard."

"Good," said Monsieur Goetzi, again, stroking his servant tenderly. "Your turn, captain."

The urchin wiped his mouth, which was stained with jam.

"Colonel," he said, making a military salute, "my hoop and I have been admitted to the skirts of three beautiful girls who are the old Countess' chambermaids. They have stuffed me with sweets and are telling me that they will require mourning-dress, like widows' weeds, because news has arrived from Vienna that the son of the house–the only son, if you please–has broken his neck like a drunkard while scaling the balcony of a young woman..."

(If I have forgotten to mention it, you will understand now that these wretches retained only the vaguest memories of their former state.)

"Is that all?" asked Monsieur Goetzi.

"No, Colonel. The three maids have given me maraschino to drink. It seems to me that I know them; but the devil take me if I can remember where I have seen them before. Here is the garrison gossip: the old woman loved her innocent of a son very much; she does not want to stay in the castle, which is full of unhappy memories. Tomorrow, she departs for Holland to find the young girl who is now her sole heir, whom she wishes to have with her. The maids have also offered me rosolio [16] ."

"And have you left your double with them?"

"Yes, he's a little drunk. They have put him in a corner with a bottle of anisette."

"Good," said Monsieur Goetzi, for the third time. "Your turn, Harpagon [17] ."

He was talking to the parrot, who was fluffing up his plumage to make himself seem larger.

"As for me, sovereign lord," old Moses replied, "my double is at this very moment with the dowager countess, who is in love with me. When she saw me fly through the open window just now, she ceased to cry and weep. She is almost consoled. I would have been able to tell you more stylishly all that the others have told you, but since that is ancient history now I will make you a more tangible gift. Take these!"

So saying, the parrot took from beneath his wing a bunch of ornately worked and gilded keys, which he respectfully placed in Monsieur Goetzi's hands, adding: "It's the old lady's key-ring. With these you can easily gain entry to her bedroom."

Monsieur Goetzi favored Jacquot [18] with a friendly pat and got to his feet, saying: "So far, so good. To work!" And he descended the sheer slope of the mountain, followed by his household.

The night was already well advanced when they arrived at the foot of the wall. In order to cross the broad moats, which were deep and filled with water, Monsieur Goetzi availed himself of the method described in the previous chapter. No sentinel raised the alarm. In the courtyard, the double of the dog Fuchs refrained from barking. All the closed doors opened to the Countess' own keys, and when they reached the antechamber where the three maids were, the maids were so absorbed in making the double of the little boy drink curaçao that they heard not a sound.

The poor dowager herself heard nothing, deafened as she was by the babble of Jacquot's double.

She was strangled by the hands of Fiole, the bald woman. Who would ever have thought that the virtuous Countess Greete could have conducted herself thus? The dog Fuchs–formerly the gentle Loos–was ordered to eat the face of the dowager, and Monsieur Goetzi sowed a beard around it.

It is rather extraordinary, but a fact, that the child was afflicted by a slight ill-feeling while he watched this ignominious treatment being meted out by his companions to one who had been his mother.

Monsieur Goetzi withdrew then, after having set fire to the bed-curtains in order to provide an explanation for the disappearance of the corpse–for I hardly need to explain that he took the unhappy Lady Montefalcone with him, and that she became the faceless innkeeper.

At the moment when Monsieur Goetzi left the castle, Fiole and her barrel disappeared from the guard-room. For their part, the three maids searched in vain for the child with the hoop, who had vanished into thin air.

The whole dismal troop, augmented by Master Haas–that was the innkeeper's name–was now traveling towards the sea. Once having reached the plain, Monsieur Goetzi turned round and was able to enjoy an imposing spectacle. The curtains had set the dowager's bed on fire, and the fire had consumed the room whose resident corpse had been taken away. It was splendid. The gorges, bizarrely illuminated, displayed the enigma of their mysterious profundity, the snowy peaks were ablaze with purple glints, and at center-stage the flames danced as wildly as a colossal torch. Our friend often told me that nothing is as beautiful as a fire in the mountains, but I cannot speak from experience.

Despite his habitual indifference to the wonders of nature, Monsieur Goetzi paused for a little while, but he soon resumed his course, crossing the Adriatic in an elegant tartan [19]. He did not stay long in Venice, so I shall not describe its carnival; *She* has devoted many pages to its astonishing magnificence. I shall only mention that Monsieur Goetzi, for his replenishment, set an infamous trap for the daughter of a Lido gondolier, and slaked his thirst with her young blood. She was completely drained.

It was during the time that Monsieur Goetzi undertook his voyage to Dalmatia that Ned Barton came to Holland to make preparations for his marriage. Count Tiberio was now living in the nice little house that he had bought in Rotterdam after the death of his wife. At the time when Ned disembarked, he still did not know of the death of his cousin, the young Count Montefalcone.

I shall not surprise you overmuch by telling you that neither Cornelia, who was fully occupied with her own affairs, nor Edward Barton had yet become aware of the relationship which existed between Tiberio and Letizia Pallanti.

It would probably be fair to say, though, that Cornelia was the only person in the whole of Rotterdam who was ignorant of the conduct of her tutor. Letizia, since her trip to Paris, had blatantly attached herself to him and her proud proclamation that "I am at home in the home of my former master" had been heard far and wide.

Things changed somewhat with the arrival of Ned Barton. You must remember that he was an Englishman–very young, to be sure, but age is immaterial. The English have a natural supremacy. His presence commanded respect and imposed a certain propriety.

Believe it or not, Tiberio was ashamed in his presence and Letizia was afraid. Their conduct reverted to its former pattern because of him, and a truce was declared in the scandal.

Ned was, however, accompanied by his domestic servant, a scatterbrained Irishman: a lazy unkempt braggart, *improper* from head to toe, who had not sixpennyworth of anything in his cramped brain but common sense.

Excessively curious, utterly indiscreet and having not the slightest sense of dignity, Merry Bones immersed himself so thoroughly in the gossip of the public house and the gutter that after a few days he knew the whole story better than those who had witnessed its unfolding.

Merry Bones could not abide Letizia Pallanti. This is invariably the way of things between valets and governesses. He had already tried more than once to spill the beans while he was shaving his young master, although Ned had not wanted to hear it, when one morning in

January–having soaped Ned's jowls–he held his razor in suspense and said: "Your honor, Holland is not a bad place, although the beer is too flat, but the Meuse will wash up more than one dead dog before March–and take my word for it, sir, your marriage is not yet made."

He whipped the razor across the hollow of his hand, suggestively.

"Be quick," Ned ordered him. "I'm in a hurry."

"The hussy's in a hurry too," the Irishman replied. "A hurry to make mischief and to do you a bad turn, or may God condemn me to eternal fire! Have you seen how she looks at you, your lordship?"

"Be quick!" Ned repeated.

"She has already devoured I don't-know-how-many thousands of that imbecile's ducats–I mean Count Tiberio–and it's no longer Miss Cornelia who has the first place at the table."

"That's true!" Edward admitted.

"Nor the best room, any longer. Holland is a pretty funny country, where schoolmistresses wear clusters of diamonds! I'll bet two sixpences–and that's a whole shilling–that I can tell you something you don't know– because, praise God, your honor never knows anything. There's a vast inheritance come down to Miss Corny, the dear angel. Her cousin Montefalcone–I'm pretty sure that's the name–who was a captain, has already gone to his death, I don't know where–and it's the governess who received the first notification of it!"

Edward at last consented to listen. "Are you sure of that, lad?"

"The telegram was from that scoundrel Goetzi."

"You've seen it, then?"

"One looks things over, don't one? It's the way to find things out."

91

"In any case," Ned said, "it's the dowager countess who will inherit from her son the captain."

Merry Bones plied his razor and removed a swathe of hair. "No doubt, no doubt, your honor," he replied, "but do you want to know what I think? The dowager countess won't make old bones. And when the dowager countess is gone, it'll be look out Miss Corny, you mark my words! Count Tiberio's business is three quarters devoured, and the governess is still hungry. Now do you understand?"

It was in this period that the letters which Ned and Corny addressed to our Anna began to lose their joyous innocence.

It was not until the end of February that the death of the grand dowager of Montefalcone–which made Cornelia a rich heiress–was confirmed. Monsieur Goetzi had returned, but he did not show himself. He had a plan, which involved provoking Edward Barton to some act of violence which would provide a pretext for calling off the marriage, but Ned did not fall into the trap which had been laid for him.

Ned had held back from confronting Signora Pallanti with the contempt that she had inspired in him, and was careful to maintain her illusions as to his true sentiments no matter how unhappy this made him.

As for Count Tiberio, Ned continued to go to his house–the only place he could meet Cornelia. Every day, Tiberio treated him more haughtily–one might almost say scornfully.

The engagement of marriage had been so public that it could hardly be broken, but it became obvious that delays were being manufactured that would be equivalent to a rupture. Thus, the matter was raised, without discussion, of a journey to Castle Montefalcone–a journey from which Edward Barton was to be excluded. And Edward Barton made no protest.

This was, at least, the impression which emerged from the letters which were read all together by our Anna, on the eve of her own wedding.

I will tell you right away that these letters were not completely sincere. They held back from revealing the whole truth–a typically English scruple. In England, we have a particular horror of the scandal called "elopement." The more freedom we give to young women within the family, the more it is incumbent upon them that they do not break their promises. Decency is an essentially English virtue. I do not believe that our Anna included a single elopement in her novels–I mean, of course, an elopement to which the young woman consented; abduction by force is a less shocking matter.

Alas, the enormity of their dread was so powerful a motive that Edward Barton and Cornelia de Witt, having searched in vain for a preferable expedient, became determined to commit themselves to that reprehensible and dangerous course of which the gentry cannot approve no matter what the excuse (although it is common enough in the lower classes). Knowing themselves to be guilty of *impropriety*, Ned and Corny kept their intention hidden from their friends.

Please do not think me capable of excusing in any degree something which is not done, but I feel bound to point out that they had to contend with an unscrupulous fraudulent bankrupt, a female living in sin and a vampire. It has to be admitted that their situation was difficult.

The Irishman Merry Bones played a considerable part in drawing them towards that evil path, but they were not in the end able to follow it, because frightful catastrophes had hastened upon them.

If they had only listened to the servant–who had, after all, a good deal of common sense–they would not have waited until the last minute; and once in London, under the protection of English law, they would have made fools of the vile bandits who simultaneously threatened their happiness, their fortune and their lives. When they finally made the decision, it was too late.

On the eve of the appointed day, the departing Letizia Pallanti treated Mademoiselle de Witt with such contempt that the poor noblewoman, bereft of prudence and patience, put her firmly in her place. On the same day–the second of February–Count Tiberio contrived at last to pick a quarrel with Edward Barton. The contract had been signed that evening. Nothing had been explicitly broken off, but when Ned presented himself at the house that evening, he was refused entry–and when Cornelia wanted to go out the following morning, she was kept prisoner.

Meanwhile, Monsieur Goetzi reappeared, playing an apparently helpful role–but you already know full well that he was not to be trusted. He gave Ned vague warning of a danger that he did not specify; he advised Corny to have courage–but he also attempted, treacherously, to drown Merry Bones in the Meuse while that good servant was guarding the boat until the hour appointed for the flight of Edward Barton and Cornelia.

You already know how the episode of the broken marriage and the interrupted flight ended. In the middle of the night, Cornelia was thrown into a carriage and taken away, not by Ned but by that infamous pair Tiberio and Letizia Pallanti, who took the overland route to the domain of Montefalcone.

PART TWO

Eight

At the very moment when Merry Bones had disappeared–in a fashion that will be revealed to you in the proper time and place–Ned, thanks to the perfidy of Monsieur Goetzi, took to the road in order to chase after his beloved and was stabbed beside the old road to Gueldre. He was then carried by villagers, dying, to the inn of *Ale and Amity.*

We can return now to that dangerous tavern where we left our Anna after the truly fantastic battle between poor Merry Bones and the double pack of subvampires who formed the household of Monsieur Goetzi, during which the clock had struck thirteen times.

After Merry Bones had left the ground-floor room, pronouncing the enigmatic words "I'm off to look for the iron coffin" everything was immediately put back in order. The various members of the Goetzi family re-entered into one another like folding chairs.

According to the laws of probability, I ought to be able to tell you that our Anna saw these impossible things with utter stupefaction, and that the mysterious phrase let fly by Merry Bones put her imagination to the torture. Well, not at all. Perhaps her spirit, by means of some exceptional facility, had already adapted itself to this kind of prodigy. Henceforth, it would require something more to astound her.

In any case, *She* became very calm.

Grey Jack was spewing forth maledictions while pressing both hands to cheeks inflamed by the slaps administered by Merry Bones, but *She* silenced him with a gesture. She recalled that Merry Bones was, after all, an Irishman, and wondered whether he might have been entirely in the wrong in the scuffle which she had just witnessed.

To tell the truth, now that things had settled down, the innkeeper and his family presented a rather peaceful appearance; one could easily assume that the bald woman, especially, was a good person. The boy brought a cup of beer to old Jack, who wet his cheeks with it and drank the remainder with pleasure.

Our Anna thought that this was a convenient opportunity to repeat the declaration that she had previously made a few minutes before the thirteenth hour.

"I demand," *She* said, in a distinct and firm voice, "to see Edward S. Barton esquire, who resides–or has resided–in this public house, if he still lives. In the unhappy event that he is deceased, whether by natural causes or in consequence of violence, I wish to be taken immediately to his resting-place, so that I can ensure that he receives the last rites, according to the provisions of the established church."

Hearing this, old Jack became tearful, while the innkeeper and his wife cried: "Ah! The dear young gentleman that God has blessed!"

For his part, the little boy said, "I've seen the dead man," and the dog howled softly, in the manner of a sick woman, while watching Anna languidly. The parrot, incessantly combing the beard of his master, repeated: "Have you dined, Ducat?"

Our Anna never could give me a full explanation of the motifs contained in these oft-repeated responses, which remain quite mysterious. Sir Walter Scott accused her of habitually leaving such explanatory gaps in her work.

The innkeeper offered her a nice room and to warm the bed therein. *She* accepted, not having slept contentedly since her departure from the cottage.

She was conducted to her apartment by the innkeeper, who brought a tea-tray, and the bald woman, who carried the candlesticks. The little fellow followed with the warming-pan and the dog brought up the rear. Grey Jack was not with them. At the time, *She* did not think to ask why she had been separated from her loyal but admittedly unintelligent servant.

I feel a little hesitant in relating this part of the story, in which our Anna's actions proved to be rather irresponsible. Should *She* really have so easily put her trust in people whom *She* had seen duplicate themselves, then sheathe themselves in the same skin, having not yet received any information about Ned? I can only point out that her greatest work, *The Mysteries of Udolpho*, is by no means lacking in similar episodes of thoughtlessness. *She* did not have a good memory, and the charming Emilia, her heroine, although endowed with extraordinary sagacity, is subject to singular fits of distraction. *She* was, moreover, overwhelmed by fatigue—and you can well imagine how terribly a young woman of good and tranquil family might be upset by adventures such as these.

The fact is that *She* got into the well-warmed bed. The bald woman carefully tucked her in; the innkeeper placed the tray containing everything necessary to make tea on the bedside table, and the little fellow set up two candles. Afterwards, they all wished her a good night and retired.

She was alone. Outside, a key grated twice as it made a double turn in the lock. The footsteps of the re-treating company faded away as they passed along the corridor. The silence would have been total had it not been for the melancholy voice of the wind plaintively shaking the window-frames.

It was the first time since her departure from her father's house that our Anna had found herself in a com-fortable situation, conducive to reverie. Her thoughts immediately turned to the pleasant countryside of Staf-fordshire. Oh how beautiful England, the gentle Queen of the World, seems when glimpsed through the tears of exile!

While *She* was dreaming in this fashion, half-asleep and in the grip of all manner of vague emotions, a dull noise came from downstairs: the harsh settlement of the clock's inner workings, which preceded the chiming of the hour. As soon as the chimes began to sound, a con-cert of wild cries and imprecations began again on the floor below, accompanied by the tumultuous echoes of a battle. The chimes sounded fourteen times, and fourteen times the scrawny bird sang cuckoo! After that, silence fell, except for the shrill voice of the little boy with the hoop, saying "I've seen the dead man!" for the final time.

That woke our Anna up with a tremendous start. The dead man was Ned! How had she contrived to for-get that cruel sorrow, even for a moment? Ned, the laughing child who had shared his early years with her and loved her as much as he was able, like a brother: Ned, the dead man!

Anna suddenly recognized the room she was in. How could *She* have failed to recognize it before? It was the room of which Ned had spoken in his letter: the one from which he had cried: "Help! Help!"

By the light of the two candles, whose long wicks emitted more smoke than flame, *She* saw the floral curtains and the set of prints depicting the exploits of Admiral Ruyter, and the round hole opposite the bed, eight feet from the floor, which had once held a stovepipe...

It was here, on this bed, that Ned had yielded up his last breath.

The candle-wicks were further elongated, crowned with black mushrooms. Their smoke filled the atmosphere with a thick and sinister fog. What was hidden within it I cannot say, but the silence was disturbed by muttering and groaning.

All the while, the obscurity became worse, for the candles became thinner and thinner and the mushrooms of their wicks grew in monstrous fashion. The half-obscured prints seemed more like distant windows, lit from without by livid fires.

Having become no more and no less than a poor superstitious child, vanquished by the terrors of midnight, *She* hid her head beneath her bedcovers.

Scarcely had *She* taken that position when she heard a noise that seemed entirely natural. It resembled the footsteps of a man wearing shoes that were too large for him. As soon as our Anna heard it, *She* regained control of herself. *She* carefully removed the bedcovers and pricked up her ears.

She had not been deceived. A heavy heel ground metallically on stonework, mere feet away from her. Our Anna's dread immediately changed its nature, although it became more than mortal. One can brave death; even the idea of dishonor, horrible as it is, is conceivable; but hobnailed boots within the bedroom of a well-brought-up young woman... The first thought that occurred to our Anna was to run to one of the windows, open it–if she were granted time to do so–and to throw herself head first into eternity.

"Begorrah!" said a voice. "They've put her in his honor's chamber! Are you asleep, Miss?"

Was it a dream? *She* thought she had recognized the voice of Merry Bones, but no matter how hard *She* looked nothing could be seen within the room.

"Is that really you, Merry?" she asked.

"Yes indeed," replied the good servant. "It's me, my pearl. Give those two candles a little blow–a Christian likes to see clearly."

You will appreciate that poor Merry was not much concerned with modesty. Our Anna blew on her candles and soon worked out why she had not been able to see the brave Irishman until now, although her eyes had searched the lighted chamber in vain. He was lodged behind the stovepipe gap as if on a balcony; he had passed two long and stick-like arms through it, and was waving them as much as he could. His strange face, straightened by masses of hair but seemingly full of good humor, was split by a smile broader than a saber-cut.

"Where have you sprung from, Merry my boy?" our Anna asked, entirely reassured.

"Well," replied Merry Bones, "didn't I tell you, miss, that I was going to look for the iron coffin?"

"What is this iron coffin?" Anna murmured.

The Irishman had disappeared from the hole now, and could be heard moving something on the other side of the wall. Immediately afterwards, the hole was plugged again. but not by the woolly head of Merry Bones. The object made a metallic sound as it scraped the inner surfaces of the hole; it only just contrived to pass through.

In the end, one last push got the object clear, and it fell noisily to the floor. The widely-grinning face of Merry Bones immediately reappeared in the bull's-eye, framed by its shock of hair.

Our Anna tried in vain to see what sort of thing it was that had made such a noise while falling. When Merry Bones was comfortably reinstalled in the gap, his two arms extended therefrom like cardboard devils from a snuffbox, he noticed her anxiety in that respect.

"I suppose you can judge how heavy it is, my flower?" he said. "That's because it's made of iron..."

"It's the coffin then!"

"...and also because it's full."

"What's inside it, for God's sake?"

"That which one usually puts in a coffin, Miss."

"A body?"

"Exactly, Miss Anna."

"Whose body?"

"My master's body, of course."

"Edward Barton's body!"

"Precisely!"

She gave a heart-rending cry.

"What? Has the devil got you?" asked Merry Bones.

Our Anna, deafened by her own sobbing, could no longer hear him. Merry Bones had to shout at the top of his voice: "I'll get it open tonight, God strike me dead if I don't. You'd do better to listen, my pearl. If there's a body in that coffin–and there is, or I'll be kippered like a herring and chewed by the black teeth of all the be-nighted Hollanders–there's a soul too, and a good soul, for all that it's an Englishman's..."

She had heard him only vaguely until then, but the last words reclaimed her attention immediately.

"What do you mean, Merry Bones?" she demanded, urgently. "Are you trying to tell me that Mr. Barton is still alive?"

"Yes, Miss–that's exactly what I mean."

"Then why isn't he moving in there?"

"He's asleep."

"Asleep!" cried our Anna, her voice rising again. "Do you think he could sleep through the coffin falling to the floor?"

"Oh, I think so,Miss–in fact, I'm certain of it."

"Do you mean that he's been narcotized?"

Merry shrugged his shoulders carelessly and said: "I don't know about narcotized, but I know that His Honor's lettuce soup was dosed with poppy heads."

I don't know if you'll approve of our Anna, but *She* told Merry Bones to stand back from the bull's-eye and, throwing her cloak about her shoulders, *She* hurried to the iron coffin, which had a lock and key just like a trunk. *She* turned the key in the lock and lifted the lid.

On seeing her cousin the midshipman lying smiling within, as fresh as Jesus in the manger, our Anna immediately became happy again. While *She* contemplated him fondly, Merry Bones reappeared at the stovepipe-hole.

"He's very pretty and very slender, isn't he, Miss?" he said. "While you're amusing yourself looking at him, you can hear me well enough, I suppose, because we haven't much time and it's necessary that you should know how all this came about.

"On the day when Miss Cornelia should have been brought away and taken to your family in England, Monsieur Goetzi–spider that he is–had already spun his web. I was caught in it and could do nothing, and what could they have done, poor little lambs, once they no longer had my help? Miss Corny was sent to the devil like a pretty little parcel, and His Honor received half a dozen knife-wounds in his side. To cut a long story short, I was a prisoner but I jumped the man set to watch me and I escaped. I arrived here, at the inn of *Ale and Amity*, yesterday evening, dying of hunger, numb with cold and in a sorry state all round. It was before your arrival, but night was falling. I was about to enter the downstairs room, without suspecting anything, when I thought it advisable to put my eye to the keyhole first. I saw the bald woman throwing poppy-heads into a pan while the innkeeper ground lettuce-hearts in a mortar. And they were both lashing out at the brat, who was asking, 'Why do you want to put the dead man to sleep?'

"As you can well imagine, I immediately got the measure of this lot, and I had no desire to walk into the middle of a wasps' nest. I went around the house looking for a back door, and when I couldn't find one I clambered up the ivy to the roof and came down the chimney-flue like a sweep. Luckily, it got me into the room where I am now. It was empty and dark, but I heard talking in the next room, which is where you are. I saw the hole where light came through and I stuffed my head into it. I saw three men–or rather, one gentleman and two halves of a rogue. It's more than likely that His Honor had already been made to drink the poppy-drugged lettuce soup, because he was asleep. He didn't seem too bad for someone who had four or five stab-wounds. Two Monsieur Goetzis were with him: the real one and his double. The real Monsieur Goetzi was laying out material inside the iron coffin, while the double was using an auger to make little holes in the side-walls.

" 'A strange occupation for a doctor of the university of Tubingen!' the double said.

" 'It's not a despicable trade,' replied the real one. 'Anyway, if I can be an upholsterer, you can be a locksmith.'

" 'And what's the point of it all, boss?'

" 'I want to get out, my son. It's my intention to retire, to live out my years in Castle Montefalcone, whose propri etors we shall become.'

"'Good idea!' said the double, rubbing his hands together. 'But how shall we become the proprietors of the lovely Castle Montefalcone?'

" 'Keep pricking–I'll explain it to you. You understand well enough that the marketplace is run by greed. On the one hand, Monsieur le Comte Tiberio Palma D'Istria has bought the young Englishman from me, dead, and I need to bring him in his coffin. Do you understand?'

" 'Perfectly.'

" 'On the other hand, Signora Pallanti has bought the same Englishman from me, but alive.'

" 'What price is Count Tiberio offering?' asked Goetzi number two.

" 'He will give me the blood of la Pallanti,' replied Goetzi number one.

" 'Oh! And *la Pallanti*?'

" 'She will give me the blood of the lovely Cornelia.'

"The eyes of both halves of the vampire sparkled as the name of the lovely Cornelia was pronounced, and their lips lit up like hot coals.

" 'All of which says nothing,' Monsieur Goetzi's double said, meanwhile, 'about our becoming proprietors of Castle Montefalcone.'

"The real Monsieur Goetzi smiled. 'When we have drunk the blood of the lovely Cornelia,' he replied, 'how can I be prevented from incorporating her? And is there any law to prevent her from keeping her true form? She will be at one and the same time Cornelia de Witt and Monsieur Goetzi. Thus, Monsieur Goetzi will be the legitimate inheritor of Montefalcone. Can you see any difficulty?'

"The other Monsieur Goetzi could find none. It was as clear as crystal. By this time, their task was complete. The iron coffin was very comfortably lined and the last auger-hole had been pierced. The two Messieurs Goetzi took hold of poor sleeping Ned, one by the head and the other by the feet, and they laid him to rest within his bier, which was then closed and the key turned thrice..."

Merry Bones then continued to recount how he had seen all this through the stovepipe hole. His ears had been flayed by the friction, but it's said that such a process is good for generating ideas and Merry Bones searched every nook and cranny of his brains for one. How could he retrieve his master from the hands of these scoundrels? While he put his brain to the torture, the true Monsieur Goetzi passed a cord around the coffin and ordered his double to open a window. A branch of the Meuse flowed beneath the window, and there was a barge waiting there, manned by two sailors.

"Ho there!" shouted Goetzi.

"Ho yourself!" came the reply from below.

"Are you ready to receive the merchandise?"

"All ready."

"Good."

The two Messieurs Goetzi lifted the coffin and hoisted it on to the windowsill. I should tell you that

Merry Bones had been forced to stand on a log of firewood to raise his head to the level of the hole in the wall–the room in which he was located served as a woodstore. His agitation caused him to make a false movement, which displaced the log. The resultant noise betrayed his presence.

The two Messieurs Goetzi immediately turned their heads and recognized him. They hissed like a pair of serpents. The inhabitants of the inn made for the room simultaneously, from every direction, and a terrible battle ensued, during which Monsieur Goetzi–the principal–continued to lower the iron coffin into the barge.

Merry Bones, being one against nine, did not have an easy time of it. Fortunately, there was a knock at the outside door of the inn. It was our Anna, with Grey Jack. The family of Monsieur Goetzi was obliged to split up, and Merry Bones was able to save himself, at the moment when the clock in the ground floor room sounded the thirteenth hour.

Once outside, he went around the building and ran after the barge which was moving down the branch of the Meuse, carrying the iron coffin. We may suppose that the two boatmen were drunk, as is usually the case, and that circumstance must have made the task of Merry Bones much easier. After several attempts, he contrived to take hold of the iron coffin and carry it back on his shoulders.

Nine

During the entire time that the Irishman was telling his story, *She* was lost in contemplation of her childhood friend.

Merry Bones shook his huge shock of hair discontentedly. "Do me the favor of closing the coffin now," he said. "You'll have fewer distractions then, and we can finish what we have to do. I have a plan–but to carry it through I need to know whether you have a cool head."

She smiled with calm pride, and lowered the lid of the coffin.

"That's good," said Merry Bones. "Now listen carefully. When I came back, I couldn't climb up to the roof, because my load was too heavy. I came in by the kitchen and I heard that pack of villains plotting in the downstairs room. This is what I gathered: at the fifteenth hour–which will soon sound, I think–Monsieur Goetzi has invited them to a little family feast. They are quite content; they believe that the coffin is heading down to Rotterdam with His Honor inside, and after the little feast of which I speak, they plan to meet up with it so that they can all leave together and deliver the merchandise to Castle Montefalcone."

"What is this little family feast?" our Anna asked.

"The drinking of your blood," replied Merry Bones.

She did not fall into a faint. "The drinking of my blood," *She* repeated, tonelessly.

"Exactly," Merry Bones replied, adding, "it's true that they prefer young women less than twenty years old; but this was how Monsieur Goetzi put it: Miss Anna Ward, if needs must, will still be potable."

"Potable!" exclaimed our unhappy friend, wringing her hands. "Potable. In God's name–potable!" I think, My Lady–and you, Sir–that you can readily imagine the various sensations which disturbed her. There are very few situations as horrible as this in the annals of modern literature. Potable!

Our Anna's first impulse was to cry: "Let's get out of here, for Heaven's sake!"

"What?" said Merry Bones. "That would be silly. It's too good an opportunity. I've found a hatchet here in the woodpile, my pearl–a hatchet for chopping wood. I've a scheme that will make us laugh. Open the coffin, take His Honor out and put him in the cupboard beside the chimney-breast...

"Hurry up! It seems to me that I hear the groaning of that evil clock, and I still need to wake that innocent Grey Jack–we have need of him."

Anna got to work briskly and courageously. *She* was strong in spite of her small stature. *She* took Edward S. Barton esquire from the coffin. lifting him in her arms. Having opened the cupboard, *She* carried him into it.

Merry Bones applauded enthusiastically. "Close it!" he said. "You have a stout heart, true enough. Now, push the coffin far enough underneath the bed to hide it completely."

She did as she was bid.

"Now," said Merry Bones, "hurry back between the sheets and pretend that you are sleeping like a pretty little angel... Begorrah! There's the mechanism grinding down below, ready to strike... when they come, don't move and don't open your eyes... bye for now!"

The movement of the clock could be heard from the floor below. The head of Merry Bones disappeared precipitously from the hole, and the first stroke of the fifteenth hour sounded, sending sonorous vibrations through the shadows of the night.

As soon as the clock's hammer rose and fell for the first time, a muffled confusion of noises emanated from the ground floor of the inn. There was the sound of footsteps on the staircase. At the second stroke, the tread of the footsteps sounded in the corridor. At the third, the door rotated slowly on its hinges, and the room was invaded by a green glow. Like the odor of felines, the glow of vampires increases at critical moments.

Monsieur Goetzi entered, alone. He had the semblance of a human shape carved out of bottle-glass. The dim candlelight streaming past him cast his shadow on the door he closed behind him. The fourth stroke rang out.

Monsieur Goetzi came directly to the bed, and our Anna's heart stopped beating. Monsieur Goetzi leaned over the bedhead. Within his body, a tumultuous voice spoke, saying: "We are thirsty! Let the feast begin!"

The clock sounded the fifth stroke.

Monsieur Goetzi pulled back the coverlet a little, his scarlet lips becoming rounded, like those of a gourmet about to taste a vintage wine, and he said with sinister gaiety: "Patience, children! I think I have the right to the first glassful."

"Then hurry, master, hurry!"

It appears that vampires have sharply-pointed tongues, with which they can make the punctures necessary for the satisfaction of their hideous appetite. Once that lancet has penetrated, they drink after the fashion of leeches.

As the sixth stroke resonated, the door opened again and Merry Bones came in, hiding his right arm behind him. The crestfallen Grey Jack followed him, as meekly as a beaten dog. An Englishman always bruises easily, and the two slaps Grey Jack had received at the thirteenth hour had, it seemed, been of the finest quality.

As soon as Merry Bones appeared, Monsieur Goetzi whistled, and his entire family emerged from his flesh at one and the same time. At a second whistle-blast, they all split into two, including Monsieur Goetzi himself—and the seventh stroke sounded.

Monsieur Goetzi immediately placed himself behind his eleven emanations, and they all threw themselves upon the Irishman. Anna, who had kept her eyes shut until then in response to Merry Bones' instruction, opened them upon the most extraordinary melee that had been seen since the world's beginning.

Two dogs, two parrots, two bald women, two little boys, two innkeepers and one Monsieur Goetzi were positively devouring the unhappy Irishman, who was only using his left hand to defend himself, and was concentrating its use on defending his eyes from the attacking parrots. He grabbed those cruel creatures by the head and twisted their necks, but that did no good at all—and while he was thus engaged, the dog and the boy sank their teeth into his legs. The innkeeper and the bald woman, aided by Monsieur Goetzi's double, tucked into his sides, his flanks, his belly and his breast.

Although he was an Englishman, Grey Jack waited on the threshold. Don't blame him for that—such were his orders. He was the reserve force, and you will understand soon enough how extremely important his role was.

The eighth, ninth and tenth chimes sounded while Merry Bones marched towards the bed, advancing inch by inch despite the relentlessness of the male and female harpies. They tore at him like a pack of hounds which have brought down their quarry; I tell you in all honesty, no part of that poor creature was spared–and he was little more than skin and bone to start with. The whole vampire troop couldn't have found more than a mouthful of meat to chew on his entire body. Skin and bones, that was what he was made of–and it's worth repeating that their stoutness provides further proof the incontestable superiority of the English.

The Irishman bled from every vein in his sorry body, and the jaws of all those jackals were reddened; but little by little he advanced nevertheless, and when the eleventh stroke sounded, there was none but one of the bald women between himself and the true Monsieur Goetzi.

Merry Bones suddenly shook his shaggy main, let loose a resounding *Begorrah!* and lifted the horrible old crone from her feet with a kick which I do not hesitate to call heroic, for the shrew became firmly lodged in the stovepipe hole. His right hand, which had not yet been shown, was abruptly brought into view. The large blade of the hatchet sparkled, and–at the very instant when the twelfth chime resonated–the head of the Goetzi-in-chief fell, severed by a single trenchant blow.

Straight away, all the other heads of an inferior order were rolling on the floor as if the same edge had separated them from their trunks.

An indescribable but mute confusion ensued. Every one ran after his or her head. In the midst of that tumultuous silence, the commanding voice of Merry Bones erupted like a thunderclap: "Your turn, Jack, you old imbecile!"

And Grey Jack proceeded to march forward in good order, without haste or idleness—as our admirable soldiers always do. His mission had already been mapped out. He drew out the iron coffin from beneath the bed and opened it, and at the very instant when the double of Monsieur Goetzi recaptured his head, Grey Jack stuffed him into the coffin and closed it, turning the key upon him.

The others were unable to perceive this, because they were fully occupied in gathering up their skulls. The thirteenth stroke sounded and the fourteenth too, while they jostled one another like vile maggots in the summer mire of a sewer. Merry Bones watched them, laughing with all his heart—which prevented him from simultaneously keeping track of the efforts of Grey Jack and Monsieur Goetzi senior.

The two of them had achieved their goals at the same time—which is to say that Grey Jack sat down on the reclosed coffin at the very moment when Monsieur Goetzi recovered his head and replaced it between his shoulders.

Monsieur Goetzi whistled. The population of vampiricules, obedient to his order, reassembled their pairs as one. At the second whistle-blast, his family performed a second maneuver, promptly re-entering into his own body—but the execution of this maneuver did not have the desired effect.

"Is anyone missing?" Monsieur Goetzi asked—but without waiting for a reply, as the clock sent forth the fifteenth stroke, he contrived to throw himself through the closed window, and disappeared into the night beyond.

A piteous voice emerged meanwhile from the iron coffin, replying: "Monsieur Goetzi! Monsieur Goetzi! It's your double that you lack!"

It was too late. The clock had finished chiming and the cuckoo sang fifteen times in its turn, while the only thing of which our poor Anna was certain was that she was still alive.

After the cuckoo's final call, Merry Bones begged for silence in order that he might explain the rest of his plan of campaign–for you will understand well enough that the war had only just begun.

"Now, Miss," he said, "it's high time that we set ourselves on the road to Castle Montefalcone, but as His Honor is fast asleep..."

"Open the cupboard door," our Anna put in, but he ignored her.

"It will be a pleasure-trip, and I don't doubt that I'll recover while we're on the road. Grey Jack will carry the coffin..."

"May the devil take you if...!" that worthy began– but Merry Bones cut the speech short, saying: "The coffin is essential to us for more than one reason; firstly to keep the bird in the cage..."

"You're mistaken, good Irishman," Monsieur Goetzi saw fit to observe, in a soft voice, from within his bier. "I'll give you my word of honor that I won't try to escape, if you let me out."

"...Secondly," Merry Bones went on, without taking the trouble to reply to this suggestion, "to introduce His Honor into Castle Montefalcone when the time comes. It seems that the walls are as high as the dome of St. Paul's, but I have my plan."

"Ah, good Irishman," said the soft voice of the coffin, "you have plenty of spirit! You are wrong to refuse my offer. I am deeply devoted to you, and I could render you excellent service."

You will doubtless suppose that this was a trap. Well, not at all! The serious authors who write thick books on vampires are in accord on this point of doctrine: a captive vampire belongs as completely to his conqueror as the same conqueror would belong to the vampire if the outcome of their contest had favored the latter.

The only differences are that ordinary men very rarely make themselves masters of vampires, the general rule of human life being that Good is always much less powerful than Evil, and the fact that having accomplished the capture of a vampire, the moral and physical inclinations of the man will prohibit his drinking the blood of the vampire.

The absence of the latter detail prevents the perfect assimilation of the vanquished vampire to his human conqueror–but the vampire prisoner is no less the slave of his new master.

While Monsieur Goetzi's double was protesting his devotion through the holes in the coffin, there was the sound of wings outside, and the window-frame was shaken from without as if a big bird or a colossal moth was bumping into the panes.

"What's that?" asked our Anna.

The prisoner immediately replied: "Don't be fooled by that for an instant. It's Monsieur Goetzi, who has come back to find me because he cannot do without me."

"I'd like to send him on his way with a bullet in the head!" cried Grey Jack. He took the stance of a man holding a rifle, firing towards the window.

"Wait, old man," said the captive. "The monster who has launched innumerable evil endeavors against your young mistress and her friends is powerless from now on. I am missing from him. It would take too long to explain the matter in precise scientific terms, but a comparison will enlighten you sufficiently. I am myself, it is true, no more than the twelfth part of Monsieur Goetzi, but I have been detached from all the rest and my absence puts them in the situation of a necklace which has lost its thread. You see his difficulty."

This had a considerable impact on the audience–but our Anna, more thoughtful than is usual in one of her tender years, asked: "Prisoner, why do you betray your patron?"

"My dear child," replied the voice of the coffin, "and don't be surprised to hear me calling you that, for I have the right; I have many reasons for acting as I do. I will tell you two of them. The first is the universal law of conquest: the subjugated remains the enemy of his vanquisher. The second, in order to be fully understood, requires me to tell you a story. In the period when Doctor Otto Goetzi came to the county of Stafford to be the tutor of Edward S. Barton, he was still only an apprentice vampire. He had neither a double nor any accessories at all. Do you remember poor Polly Bird, the daughter of the High Farm, whose premature death set the whole parish mourning three years ago? Well, my friends, it is the unfortunate Polly Bird herself who is speaking to you. Monsieur Goetzi, when he received from Peterwardein the diploma of a master vampire, immediately chose me to be his double and the foundation of his interior mechanism."

"When I think," our Anna exclaimed, "that we have sat one beside the other in church, with the seven Bobington girls!"

Merry Bones had understood that Grey Jack would not easily submit to carrying the coffin. "All things considered," he said, "Polly Bird was a pretty good girl then, and the mistress has no chambermaid. If Polly will promise us to be good, and to carry the coffin, I don't see why we shouldn't amuse ourselves by putting up with her until we get to Castle Montefalcone."

Polly Bird prevailed. Merry Bones inserted the key into the iron coffin's lock and opened it. Monsieur Goetzi–for it was still Monsieur Goetzi–could now be seen, looking at the company in a sweet and modest fashion. On careful consideration, however, Anna and the others were able to perceive, behind the features of the despicable doctor, something of the physiognomy of Polly Bird.

The unfortunate thanked them profusely, curtsying as soon as she had been set on her feet. We shall employ the feminine gender in speaking of her henceforth, in order to avoid confusion with the real Monsieur Goetzi. You should not forget, however, that this was a man–and in consequence of that fact, the plan to confer upon her the position of chambermaid to our Anna had to be abandoned.

What is more, as a security measure, the coffin was attached to her neck by a strong chain. In the first place, Grey Jack and Merry Bones ensured by this means that she would carry it; in the second place, it seemed reasonable to suppose that the restriction of her movements imposed by such a cumbersome burden would make any attempt to escape very difficult.

Ten

Dawn was breaking when *She* dismissed her companions so that she could attend to her *toilette*. In the meantime, the former Polly set about waking Ned Barton, by means which I cannot explain. When our Anna rejoined her companions–having offered up a brief prayer, or at least made the appropriate gestures, in order to request divine protection from further perils–Ned had just opened his eyes and was looking around in a stupefied manner.

"Where am I?" he asked, at once.

She wanted to give him a full explanation, but Merry Bones insisted that they get underway immediately. "I have had a chat with our companion Polly," he said. "She has given me some good advice. We have a rather delicate task to complete before we head for Castle Montefalcone. While the real Monsieur Goetzi remains alive, nothing else matters."

They went downstairs. They saw that the clock in the ground floor room had stopped at exactly fifteen o'clock. The cuckoo had vanished.

As soon as they had crossed the threshold, their eyes were caught by a large placard suspended beneath the lantern. The sign read: *INN TO LET*.

Without pausing to contemplate this curious but unimportant detail, the little caravan took to the road. The former Polly was in the front rank, closely guarded to the right and the left by Grey Jack and Merry Bones. As agreed, Polly carried the iron coffin. Anna and Ned Barton–who was still a little weak and needed the support of his companion's arm–brought up the rear. The Dutch, being a ponderous race, watched indifferently as they passed by.

118

Their journey to the banks of the Rhine would have been incident-free were it not for some vague whistling sounds heard above the sound of the wind, and some confused movements in the bushes. Having been warned by the ex-Polly, who was anxious to display her perfect loyalty, Merry Bones explained to our Anna that Monsieur Goetzi was dispersed in the air and in the water behind the foliage, lying in wait for a suitable moment to recapture the double who was indispensable to his freedom of movement.

Once, our Anna felt something like a child's hoop brush her legs, and a shrill voice emanating from who knows where said: "There's the dead man!"

Having reached the Rhine, they hired a boat to take them upriver as far as Cologne. Towards evening, when the shadows of twilight descended upon the Rhine and its banks, a pale green glow appeared some two hundred yards in front of the boat. It followed the watercourse upriver, moving at exactly the same speed as the boat.

As the darkness deepened, the glow became brighter. It gradually became concentrated; having formerly been widespread, it eventually appeared no larger than a man's body. Now, Monsieur Goetzi could be distinctly seen, sailing feet first, shrouded by his vivid aureole.

While each of them silently considered this strange spectacle, the former Polly broke down in tears. When she was asked why she was so sad, she replied: "Do you think that I can look upon the monster who stole my honor and my happiness without being overcome by rage? Mark this: he will not give you an inch of leeway while you lack the means of destroying him utterly. I tell you this partly for the sake of my vengeance, but above all else for your safety. Every hour of the day and night,

119

whether he be apparent or hidden, you may be certain that Monsieur Goetzi is always prowling around you. Consequently, I now intend to explain in every detail the plan which I have already suggested briefly to Merry Bones–which, if it is executed courageously, will permanently annihilate our common enemy. The moment is favorable, for while we can see him down there, we can be certain that he is not here, listening. While he does not have me, he is obliged to keep all his other parts within him, and you will understand how angry that makes him."

That response having silenced all objections, they gathered closely around the former Polly, each one paying close attention–except perhaps Edward S. Barton esquire. It pains me to say it, but the young midshipman was not yet fully recovered. He was still dazed and confused, in need of time and tender care.

The unfortunate who had been Monsieur Goetzi's first victim unburdened herself in this manner: "There is a little-known place which is undoubtedly the strangest in the world. The people who inhabit the barbarous lands around Belgrade sometimes call it Selene, sometimes Vampire City, but the vampires refer to it among themselves by the names of the Sepulchre and the College. It is normally invisible to mortal eyes–and to the eyes of each of those who contrive to catch a glimpse of it, it presents a different image. For this reason, reports of its nature are various and contradictory.

"Some tell of a great city of black jasper which has streets and buildings like any other city but is eternally in mourning, enveloped by perpetual gloom. Others have caught sight of immense amphitheaters capped with domes like mosques, and minarets reaching for the sky more numerous than the pines in the forest of Dinawar.

Yet others have found a single circus of colossal proportions, surrounded by a triple rank of white marble cloisters lit by a lunar twilight that never gives way to day or night.

"Arranged there, in mysterious order, are the sepulchral dwellings of that prodigious people which the wrath of God has placed in the margins of our world. The sons of that people, half demon and half phantom, are living and dead at the same time, incapable of reproducing themselves but also deprived of the blessing of death. Their womenfolk are ghouls, also known as oupires. Some, it is said, have sat on thrones and terrified history. Following the example of those men of iron who were oppressors of the country in the Middle Ages–and who, when beaten back, retreated to their impregnable fortresses–they maintain this sinister and splendid shelter: a citadel and place of refuge, as inviolable as the tomb.

"Every time a vampire is severely injured, in a manner that we would deem mortal were we speaking of an ordinary human being, he makes for the Sepulchre. Their existence can undergo crises which are not actually death, but which resemble it. They have been found, in various parts of the world, reduced to the state of a cadaver, although the flesh remains uncorrupted and a mechanism set within the heart continues to secrete a warm ruby-red liquor. In this state, a vampire is at the mercy of his discoverer. He can be chained and walled up. He can make no move to defend himself until chance brings his plight to the attention of an evil priest who holds a key–a key which is the only means by which the workings of their apparent life can possibly be restored. To achieve this, the priest introduces the key into the hole which every vampire has in the left side of his breast, and he turns...

"Monsieur Goetzi is in exactly this situation; he is in pressing need of rewinding. As time continues to run out, he will be subject to a gradual but increasingly rapid enfeeblement, until he can obtain the requisite number of turns of the key. He is already on his way to the Sepulchre; only the passionate desire to recover me–his missing link, his synovia [20], if I may be permitted to use the scientific term which he applies to me himself–forces him to remain close to us. While he still feels that his health is not too poor, he will make no move, waiting for a favorable moment to whisk me away by force or stealth...

"Come closer, I beg you, for a fog is beginning to form, and Monsieur Goetzi's glow can hardly be seen any longer. Be sure that as soon as he can approach us without being seen, he will slip into the body of one of our oarsmen...

"We are also headed for the Sepulchre. Don't worry that it will take us out of our way; it only requires a slight detour. I know the byways of that funeral hospital by heart. We will go in as far as Monsieur Goetzi's hidey-hole, and then...but the green glow is no longer perceptible. Look out!"

"What?" said our voyagers, all at the same time. "What shall we do then?"

"Shh!" said the former Polly, putting a finger to her lips. "Listen!"

A suspicious splashing agitated the water around the boat, whose wash was brightened by a pale light.

"Tell us in a whisper," begged our Anna.

The former Polly agreed. She was a truly good girl, although that appearance was hidden by the features of

Monsieur Goetzi. One by one, they lent her their ears and received her murmurous confidence.

"Excellent!" they cried, one and all. "That idea is worth its weight in gold."

Do you remember the burst of laughter which our Anna heard while disembarking, on the night of her arrival at Rotterdam? Something similar grated in the air, and at the same time, one of the oarsmen gave a sudden start.

"Look out!" commanded the ex-Polly. "The enemy is here! You have only one means of keeping me safe, and the fact that I tell you what it is will give you the measure of my good faith. Put me back in the iron coffin, and sit on top of it!"

They had no sooner moved to act on this suggestion than the possessed oarsman made another convulsive movement, releasing a huge sigh. At the same time, a sound like that of a body falling into the water was heard. Monsieur Goetzi, realizing that his strategy had scant chance of success, had gone back whence he had come.

The rest of the night passed peacefully.

The new day dawned while they were passing through Dusseldorf. Our Anna asked Merry Bones to find a shop selling musical instruments and buy a lute– which served, in spite of the circumstances, to relieve the monotony of their journey.

Monsieur Goetzi seemed to have disappeared; they were able to reopen the coffin to let a little air in to the unfortunate Polly.

At Cologne they abandoned the Rhine for the overland route, hiring a coach for that purpose. They crossed

Westphalia, Hesse, part of Bavaria and took to the water again at Ratisbonne, this time on the Danube.

Nothing noteworthy occurred between Ratisbonne and Linz, between Linz and Vienna, between Vienna and the ancient Magyar city of Ofen–which is nowadays called Buda–or between Buda and the plains of southern Hungary.

It was one morning thereafter that our Anna and her companions saw the thick-waisted towers of Peterwardein set before the magical skyline of Belgrade, bathing in the glorious scintillation of the first light of the Oriental sun. Open countryside extended to the horizon on either side, perfumed by corn and flowers, through which the broad Danube flowed like a sea.

Since Vienna, there had been no sign to indicate the presence of Monsieur Goetzi, but the former Polly had never ceased to say: "He is there." And, indeed, in the last hours of their voyage, he became perceptible again, still floating feet-forwards, enveloped by a small cloud of pale fog–but he was considerably smaller, and so very thin! The livid haze which surrounded him flickered as if it were on the point of vanishing.

At some distance from Belgrade, he steered for the shore and made landfall in the reeds, seeming to be little more than a thin puff of smoke.

"The abominable villain is powerless now," said the former Polly, placing her hands on her good heart.

It was on the Christian bank of the Danube that Monsieur Goetzi had taken to the land, not far from Semlin in the banate of Timisoara. He could still be seen beyond the reeds for a moment, but then was lost in the tall verdure of a cornfield.

"We must land!" said Polly, who was now the leader of the expedition.

The boat immediately moved to the bank. They climbed ashore. Polly, taking her place at the head of the column, immediately headed for the little town of Semlin, the nearest to the Turkish border.

"Now that my infamous seducer is reduced to the last extremity," she said, marching rapidly, "he will undoubtedly be couched within his marble trough, for the Sepulchre is closer to us than you imagine. Now that we have no further need to beware of his espionage, I can fill in the last details of my plan. We have arrived at the terminus of our journey. When the hour is propitious, we shall be able to see the unique atmosphere which surrounds and veils Selene, the dead city. At present, the morning is too bright–and I am glad of it, because we must have time to make our preparations.

"You know that vampires divide the day into twenty-four equal parts, and that their clock-faces consequently show twenty-four hours. At the twenty-third hour–which is to say, at eleven o'clock in the morning–the mercy of God has allowed that their power is in abeyance for sixty minutes, as shown by the hands of the clock. This is their great secret, and by revealing it I expose myself to the risk of the most abominable tortures–but I'm prepared to do it, in order to achieve my vengeance. It's now about eight o'clock; we shall have three hours in Semlin, during which we must buy charcoal, a portable stove, bottles of Epsom salts and a box of candles. Don't ask me why–you shall see the utility of these various objects for yourselves. We also need a skillful surgeon, and I know just the one: Magnus Szegeli, the most learned practitioner for miles around. He will want nothing more than to follow us, for he has a score to settle with the vampires. Unhappily, I cannot take care of that matter myself."

"Why not?" asked our Anna.

"Because, Miss, Monsieur Goetzi has drained two charming young ladies whom he adored, and who comprised his entire family. Given that I am manifest in the form of Monsieur Goetzi, Doctor Szegeli could scarcely fail to recognize me, and you will understand that I would hardly inspire confidence in him."

She turned away, unable to conceal her repugnance, and murmured: "Unhappy creature! Have you tasted the blood of those poor girls?"

"In our condition, Miss," replied Polly, lowering her eyes, "one cannot do other than one must."

"And did you find it good?" asked Edward Barton, as curious as any seaman.

Perhaps for the first time, *She* thought of her fiancé with pride. William Radcliffe would never have asked such an unwarranted question.

Semlin, which is the ancient domain of Malavilla–a prize frequently taken and retaken by the infidels in the Middle Ages–still harbors the remains of the fortress built by John Hunyadi [21] . There our companions bought the various objects which would be indispensable to them, and our Anna had the idea of furnishing herself with a sketch-artist. *She* thought of everything. It is unfortunate that photography had not yet been invented.

The Slavonian surgeon Magnus Szegeli lived next to the Israelite school. Our Anna went into the house alone, while Ned Barton, Jack, Merry Bones and the unhappy Polly devoted themselves to the vulgar necessity of taking their morning meal.

Doctor Szegeli was still a young man, although his hair was entirely white. His figure, ravaged by pain, displayed the legacy of the deplorable history of his two daughters. Almost as soon as *She* began speaking–at the first word which informed him that he was required to fight vampires–he snatched up his case and brandished it with all the eagerness that the hope of vengeance inspires. Following Polly's advice, *She* also persuaded him to bring one of those large iron ladles used in poor houses to serve soup, having first sharpened its edges. The purpose of this instrument will be revealed to you in due course.

It is as well to put on record that the number of young women devoured by vampires in the immediate environs of their convent was much less considerable that one might have imagined. In order not to rouse the entire country to revolt, the vampires had agreed between them that they would not inflict any damage within a perimeter of fifteen leagues. Monsieur Goetzi had, therefore, broken this pact in slaking his thirst to the detriment of an inhabitant of Semlin–a prohibited town, like Peterwardein and Belgrade. In consequence, for fear of being reprimanded by his own kind, he had not dared enroll the two Szegeli girls in his company of slaves and had made mere art-objects out of their carefully-prepared cadavers.

When our Anna rejoined her companions, she found that Polly was once again enclosed in the iron coffin–a doubly useful precaution, firstly because the Slavonian surgeon would be unable to recognize Monsieur Goetzi in her, and secondly to spare the unfortunate girl any temptation to flight or treason. Her repentance seemed sincere, it is true–but she had, after all, acquired some exceedingly nasty habits whilst in the company of her ancient master.

They departed on the stroke of ten o'clock–the twenty-second hour, according to the clocks of the Sepulchre. The weather was bright. Semlin, which is on the line of latitude which passes between Venice and Florence, has the same gentle climate as Italy. Our voyagers went gravely and silently across fields of millet and corn, whose hedges were made of oleander. She marched ahead, followed by Grey Jack and Merry Bones, who carried the coffin. Edward S. Barton esquire came next, carrying the charcoal, the stove and the box of candles. Doctor Szegeli brought up the rear, his paces moderated by grief. Don't think that I've forgotten the painter; he wandered away to the left and the right, as is an artist's prerogative.

Ordinarily, supernatural phenomena manifest themselves around midnight, under cover of complete darkness. If you will permit me to make the observation, Milady–and you, Sir–the episode I am describing, with due historical rigor, presents a remarkable character of originality. It was the middle of the day and the sun bathed the natural world with its bluest radiance. No delusion was possible.

At three-quarters of a league from Semlin, in the direction of Peterwardein, the terrain underwent an abrupt change of appearance. No more oleanders could be seen, nor laburnums, nor lilacs. The rich verdure of green corn disappeared. The soil, so rich a moment ago, became dull, as if recently showered by ash. At the same time, the blue of the sky was veiled with grey, and something for which there was no word–a melancholy screen–was drawn across the face of the sun.

These symptoms became exaggerated with surprising rapidity. After five minutes, it seemed to our voyagers that they were separated by an enormous distance from the objects which had formerly surrounded them. They closed ranks instinctively, forming into pairs and searching the sky for the sun which had been hidden behind the falseness of that night.

"Go on," said Polly, within the coffin.

And they went, although their limbs were weakening, their heads unquiet and their bosoms oppressed by an uncanny weight. They staggered and bumped into one another. You would have thought that they had become heavily inebriated–or, rather, that they had suddenly been struck blind; for what surrounded them now was utter, impenetrable darkness.

"Go on!" said the voice of the coffin.

They went. Is there some darkness even deeper than the blackest night? That something fell upon them, as cold as a pall. All external sound had died away. Nature was no longer breathing.

In the midst of the nameless silence, the voice of the coffin spoke: "Stop!"

They obeyed. Suddenly, beside them–among them, I should rather say, so tightly did the sound enwrap them–a bell that sounded loudly, but as clearly as the note of a harmonica, slowly tolled the twenty-third hour.

At the twenty-third stroke, the shadows were rent apart and the Sepulchre appeared.

The company was in the very center of Vampire City.

Eleven

The desolate city which surrounded our friends was entirely devoid of life, color and movement. Their spirits
were overwhelmed by the silence and the spectral splen-
dor of its marvelous scenery, whose melancholy richness
was unparalleled and indescribable. Magnificent beneath
the malediction of God, the city had been named Selene
after the Greek goddess of the moon; most experts agree
that the moon may be assigned to the vampire race as a
fatherland.

Let's begin with the central edifice, situated in the
middle of a vast circular plaza. Imagine an immense ro-
tunda where the styles of antique architecture are aggregated one above the other in the service of a barbaric but
learned fantasy, audaciously marrying the strangest ar-
chaisms of Assyria with dreamlike *Chinoiserie* and
Hindu caprice. This was a temple, a tower, a gargantuan
Babel constructed in pale porphyry, delicately tinted
with a hesitant and dilute shade of green. Huge blocks of
this stone, lusterless and yet as translucent as amber,
were bound together by narrow seams of black marble.

The first section of the peristyle set around a circular flight of thirteen steps was composed of Doric columns, as thick as those of the temple at Paestum, but so
large in proportion that they produced an impression of
cyclopean solidity. Between the columns appeared
Moresque windows with wildly excessive arches. The
second series was Ionic, to the extent that the designa-
tions reserved by historians of art to characterize the exaggerated formulas of barbarism can be applied to it. It
was equipped with trefoil windows. The third was cor-
rugated by Corinthian columns and retreating walls,

pierced by flattened Gothic arches. The fourth was Composite, but floridly displayed thousands of strangely regular ornamentations, shielding windows in the form of stars. The fifth and last was an efflorescence of veined colonnettes, a fountain of pearl-encrusted lianas, which supported a vaulted roof, partly leveled-off and crowned by another, smaller cupola from which a fountain of flames shot forth. It played with all the styles, denying all precepts and defiantly displaying the impossibilities of Faerie.

But what defined the character of the whole of that colossal chapel–at once grandiose and frivolous, magnificent but woebegone–was the inordinate protrusion of its capitals and their entablatures. The friezes and cornices of the Doric flared out; the volutes of the Ionic were swollen and extended; the acanthus leaves of the Corinthian and the Composite erupted in cascades; and the hectic vegetation of the final nameless order formed a huge and deep sheltering ladder, disposed in parasols which gave the ensemble a pagoda-like profile.

Under the peristyle, between each pair of columns, there was a crouching porphyry tiger, its claws tearing open the heart of a supine young woman.

Twenty-four pedestals were ranged atop the circular flight of steps, also mounted with statues of young women–all of them very beautiful, but every one assaulted, subdued and violated by an invisible enemy.

These statues bordered a large circular arena which filled in the heart of the rose beyond whose openings the six main squares of the Vampire City, with their subsidiary streets, were set. Each of these districts seemed enormous, packed to the limit of vision with innumerable buildings whose perspectives were lost in an opal haze. They were all different, but their design exploited clever analogies which persuaded the eye that they were in perfect harmony.

All this livid magnificence was redolent with death; it was soundless, motionless and breathless. Even the air seemed eternally asleep, undisturbed by the slightest whisper of wind. The grandeur of the necropolis was overpowering; words could not express its terrible solitude.

Although the gigantic assemblies of architectural marvels testified to the might of the hand of man, there was no one here. There was not even a shadow to be seen in the white expanses which stretched into the distance in every direction, nor beneath the colonnades which curved around them. The pallid blooms of all these flower-beds slept on their stems, unswayed by any breeze. The enchantment which had suspended their animation had power enough to freeze the water-jets of fountains in mid-air. You know how monotony enlarges everything by discouraging thought, even immensity itself; twilight as cold and clear as the face of the moon struck that symmetrical crowd of monuments–all built of the same stone, colorless and semi-transparent–from every side at once, casting not a single shadow.

Within the majesty of silence and death, there was a fugitive impression of wakefulness. In the debauchery of styles and the wild promiscuity of decorations, there was an orgiastic savor. The orgy was temporarily suspended– but who would want to be in that sepulchral Babylon at the hour when it was resumed?

The chimes of the crystal bell reverberated for a long time in the mute atmosphere.

The newcomers stood still, lost in astonishment. While our Anna tried in vain to measure these frightful marvels, Merry Bones muttered Celtic imprecations and

Grey Jack peered into the distance in the vague hope that he might be able to discover the sign of a tavern somewhere in the depths of the panorama. The artist had taken up his crayons. Doctor Szegeli, the distraught father, studied the statues of young women with a moist eye.

"Let's go! Let's go!" said Polly Bird within the coffin. "There isn't time to waste in trifling. We have to get on! Monsieur Goetzi resides in the Serpent Quarter. Forward!"

At the entrance to each main square was a pedestal supporting the image of an animal, from which the quarter took its name. Merry Bones took the lead again, and having found the statue of the serpent, he set a course between the two ranks of mausolea indicated thereby.

When they had passed through the gateway into the square, the impression of immensity overwhelmed our Anna's mind as she was confronted by streets radiating in every direction, grafted on to other streets, while the principal thoroughfare plunged into vertiginous depths.

Each tomb, viewed at close quarters, was a considerable monument. Some, doubtless enclosing members of the vampire nobility, had the proportions of royal palaces–and there were not merely hundreds of them, but thousands! Each mausoleum bore a name, inscribed in black letters beneath its main entrance. The majority of these names were unfamiliar, but some could be found among them whose presence in that place explained many enigmas posed by the history of ages past, and also by that of the present: the names of evil misers whose scandalous wealth is the misery of entire nations; the names of courtesans, the obscene ruination of morals and patrimonies; and the names of those glorified by the title of "conqueror" in imbecilic poetry and slavish art because they crushed the weak by force and cemented their renamed atrocities with tears, shame and blood!

More than once, while passing before one of these ostentatious temples, where some illustrious scourge of humanity lay asleep, our Anna wanted to go in–but every time, the voice of Polly Bird, impatient and quivering with fear within the coffin, would cry: "Make haste! It's a matter of life and death, and we have little time!"

They hurried on, but the road seemed endless. Streets were followed by more streets, tombs by more tombs, and on they went. They did not encounter a single living creature in that interminable journey.

Finally, however, Polly, who was keeping track of their road through the holes in the coffin, said: "We are nearly there. Hold me hard, for although I hate my master, his heart attracts me as a magnet draws iron, and I may try in spite of myself to throw myself into him." The noise of her writhing, as she bruised her sides against the iron walls, could indeed be heard from within the coffin.

"Halt!" she said, at last. "We have arrived. Here it is."

Monsieur Goetzi was neither a king, nor a dictator, nor a tribune, nor a humanist philosopher, nor the founder of a finance house. He was no Baron Iscariot or Baroness Phryne; he could not pretend to be part of the vampire aristocracy. He was a mere doctor, although he did not practice medicine. For this reason, his tomb was so shabby that comparison with the patrician sepulchres almost excited compassion. It was a meager chapel in the barbaric Greek style, only a little grander than St Paul's in London.

Its architecture was a trifle parsimonious, comprising no more than four or five hundred columns. It was ignominiously overshadowed on one side by the mausoleum of a Prussian prime minister, and on the other by the cathedral of an ancient Parisienne whose practice had been–and would continue to be–to drink the blood of imbeciles, making no discrimination between the sons of the virtuous and the sons of the villainous, provided that they had gold in their veins and plenty of servants.

At the center of the facade, on a tablet of black jasper, the name of Monsieur Goetzi stood out in feebly illuminated pale green letters, accompanied by several Greek characters.

Γωεθεε

Our Anna regretted that she did not have William Radcliffe on hand, who read Greek as well as a Turk. She was obliged to ask the surgeon Magnus–who explained to her, in spite of his grief, that the name seemed to be formed from two distinct roots, one derived from the noun *earth* and the other from the verb *to boil*.

"Volcano!" cried our Anna. "A good name for a scourge of mankind!"

"Open it and go in!" ordered Polly, still restless within the coffin. "Even a single moment's delay might expose us to the most frightful misfortune."

They went up the steps and through the peristyle. The great door was not locked, and they went in. A long nave extended into the interior of the tomb, flanked by a regal cloister, above which ran a double tier of galleries, the whole being capped by a Byzantine cupola. All the walls, pilasters and arches were made of that semi-transparent amber-tinted stone that our Anna called "lunar." In front of the columns there was a closely-packed series of statues, all representing young women, which made a circle around a porphyry shell precisely positioned in the center of the nave.

All these young women extended their softly rounded arms towards the shell, collectively bearing an endless wreath. Before them, a rank of Ninevite tripods was set, supporting alabaster bowls in which some unknown liquor was burning, so pale that the spirituous flame seemed ruby-red against its background.

Within the central shell, Monsieur Goetzi was lying on his back with his arms tightly pressed to his sides. The miserable wretch was reduced almost to nothing: diminished, emaciated and shriveled like a damp parchment dried by the sun.

"O my dear master," cried Polly, performing extravagant contortions within her iron box, "were I not a prisoner, how joyfully I would come to your aid." But she added, without pausing for breath: "Go on! Don't delay! Tear out his heart–without making him suffer too much!"

I ask your permission now to use a rather offensive word; circumstances demand it. Nothing stinks like a vampire who is at rest in the freedom of his own house. Despite the numerous cassolettes which were burning, Monsieur Goetzi, now seriously inconvenienced, exhaled an odor so malignantly fetid that our companions would have been at risk of death by asphyxiation had it not been for the bottles of Epsom salts bought in Semlin. That was why Baroness Phryne made the fortune of so many perfume manufacturers!

Doctor Szegeli took up his bundle, but his hand trembled lamentably, and you will understand why when I tell you that the unhappy father had recognized his two daughters among the statues.

"Go on! Go on!" repeated Polly, "Every minute is worth a century. Destroy the heart of my unfortunate master, quickly and gently!"

Merry Bones was only an Irishman, but he was not afraid of work. He snatched the bundle from Magnus' hands and said: "May the Devil choke me if I can't cut out what needs to be cut. I've been a butcher's boy in Galway, so I'll do the honors."

"Go on, my boy!" said the voice of the coffin. "Finish the job, but do him no harm!"

Merry Bones rolled up his sleeves. Our Anna, deeply moved, gravely took up a position from which she could see more clearly. Edward Barton and Grey Jack stood watch over the coffin, which threatened to fly open at any moment. Doctor Szegeli stayed beside Merry Bones lest his advice should be required to direct the operation.

The young Slavonian painter, seated on his folding chair, made a sketch.

I would, of course, be embarrassed were I to describe with technical exactitude the surgical operation which was carried out. Perhaps, too, it would exceed the bounds of decency. It is sufficient for you to know that Monsieur Goetzi kept his eyes open and fixed throughout the operation. His body remained immobile, because it was reduced to such a pitiably meager state.

"If he had only been given twenty-four hours," said Polly, "my dear master would have been plump and fresh. Cut away! Cut deep! Oh, I am so deeply attached to him!"

When the patient's chemise was drawn apart, everyone could see a little round opening, like the one in the end of a quill, on the left side of his breast. Ruby-red blood was coursing therefrom, drop by drop.

At the moment when the mysterious mechanism of vampiral vegetation was uncovered and displayed, the cupola began to vibrate with sound and the walls, galleries and cloister acquired a voice. They made a kind of plaintive music as pale as the ambient light, the marble of the edifice and the uncertain flames flickering in the cassolettes.

Merry Bones plied the scalpel conscientiously and proved his talent for butchery. But beneath the slicing edge of the blade, not a single drop of blood sprang forth. Evidently, nothing but the heart itself was alive; its envelope was dead and dry.

"Pay attention, please!" said Polly. "My life is attached to that of my master by a small thread of nervous tissue, which you must cut before touching the heart. You will find eleven such threads in the pericardium: one for each of my co-accessories. My own thread is the first on the right. Can you see it?"

"I see it," replied Merry Bones, severing it delicately.

The former Polly received such a shock in consequence that the iron coffin jumped into the air. Meanwhile, the heart was completely exposed, redder than a cherry and in a perfect state of freshness. Our Anna, pressing her bottle to her nostrils, examined it curiously. She never neglected an opportunity to further her education.

"Is the stove getting hot?" asked Polly.

"Yes," replied Ned and Jack, who had been ordered to see to it.

"Then goodbye, master! I will weep long and hard for you... Take it out!"

Merry Bones took from Doctor Szegeli the iron ladle which had been sharpened with this object in mind and, adroitly inserting it beneath the heart, drew the organ out intact.

Monsieur Goetzi's eyes became dull.

The monumental music vibrating within the blocks of porphyry swelled up as if in a mighty groan.

"Quickly!" cried Polly. "Grill it! Burn the heart of my seducer! But above all, do not lose the ashes, for I fear that we shall have dire need of them. What time is it?"

Our Anna consulted her watch, whose hands stood at a quarter to noon.

"Everything depends on your swiftness," said Polly. "The route from here to the central square is long, and there is only the one exit. Turn up the heat!"

The heat was turned up. Everyone set themselves to blow on the charcoal within the furnace, and the heart of the vampire was placed on the brazier, where it soon began to crackle and smoke. Then it burst into flame. It burned like a plum pudding doused in rum–and while it did so, the body of Monsieur Goetzi dwindled within the shell. His eyes, animated by a horrid urgency, rolled and rolled.

The ladle became red hot. Merry Bones held on to it with the aid of his jacket, which he moistened and folded round the handle. The others continued to blow, urged on by the voice of the coffin.

The heart was reduced to ashes. That which remained of Monsieur Goetzi within the shell was an exceedingly scanty residue of transparent matter, within which a series of little dead things could be distinguished: a parrot, a dog, a bald woman, a bearded inn-keeper and a little boy with a hoop.

The livid music had ceased to make itself heard. The cold flames had expired within the cassolettes. The statues of young women, having fallen noiselessly from their pedestals, were lying in the porphyry dust which made up the ground–and all around the vault, a great black cuckoo like that of the Dutch clock flew in circles, fervently beating its silent wings.

"The matter is concluded," said Polly, who had fully recovered her tranquillity in the depths of the coffin. "I had a moment of vertigo, but it has passed. Now we must get out of here. You must have heard the saying of Doctor Samuel Hahnemann, who invented the doctrine of homeopathy: when I am well, I have no faith in medicines–but it's sure and certain that the best remedy to employ against vampires is the ashes of a vampire. Take two or three pinches of that of my master to serve our present purpose, and keep the rest in the ladle. What's the time now?"

"Four minutes to noon," was the reply.

"Forward! Shift your legs! Carry me!"

They left the monument at once, leaving the furnace and the sack of charcoal, for which they had no more use. Edward S. Barton and the hired painter carried the iron coffin, because Merry Bones had been ordered to protect their retreat by means of the soup-ladle containing the ashes of Monsieur Goetzi's heart. Don't smile: you shall soon see the extraordinary power of that medicament.

As far as Magnus Szegeli was concerned, the unhappy father had decided to carry the statues of his two daughters. Unable to manage it, because they were too heavy, he threw himself back upon the residue of Monsieur Goetzi and took time out to trample it within its container and subject it to the most shameful outrages. *She* had not the heart to blame him for that futile but legitimate vengeance.

They emerged into the street. Outside, all was as mute and immobile as before—but something had modified the uniform tint of the splendidly lugubrious vista. As the moment of awakening approached—the dawn before the night, as it were—mysterious lights and shadows sprang up among the ghastly enormities: colors endeavoring to be born. There was a hint of red in the depths of the pallid atmosphere, and the silence was confused by murmurs...

Our companions ran full tilt through the streets of Selene, incessantly urged on by the exhortations emerging from the depths of the iron coffin, where Polly rendered herself as breathless as a jockey at Epsom. In truth, they could already see that she was not at all in error. The murmur spreading through the silence was becoming louder; the vague red gleam was increasing in intensity; and the wingbeats of the great black cuckoo which circled above the fleeing company were beginning to make themselves heard.

At the moment when our friends reached the gateway marked with the statue of the serpent, that magnificently proportioned porphyry animal began slowly to uncoil, and its previously colorless semi-diaphanous scales acquired an indescribably rich green tint.

At that very moment, a vast rumble emitted by the principal dome filled the space with a series of harmonious vibrations, and all the immobile pallors which stretched to the horizon of the dead city in every direction came to life, flooded by an intensely vivid green hue. The lines tracing the junctions of the stones, which had been black, took on a scarlet tint like long zigzags of fire.

It was magnificent, but horrible–and as this sinister grandeur, darkening and reheating the limitless horizons, submerged thought in a sea of terror, Polly said: "Faster! Run! Your death-knell is about to toll, and you must flee! What's the time?"

"One minute to noon."

"Run! Run for your lives!"

They ran, panting, staggering, bathed by a cold feverish sweat which trickled from their burning bodies. They were in the middle of the central plaza when the crystal bell bestirred itself to sound the first chime of the twenty-fourth hour. The black bird beat its wings and launched a triumphant "cuckoo" into the air. From the top to the bottom of the great church, the open windows released a furnace-like glow which seemed gradually to embrace the entire atmosphere, while the deep green of the walls and columns was checkered with lines of fire.

The young women of the peristyle were writhing and screaming now beneath the claws of the tigers; the statues assumed lascivious poses upon their illuminated pedestals. Shadow and light, night and day, grace and terror were all mingled therein, confounded by infernal promiscuity. It was no longer a dream, nor a nightmare, nor a hallucination; it was the debauch of all those re-united entities, their battle and their tempest.

The bell of crystal continued to sound, and after each chime the black bird loosed its cry, which grew ever louder. In like manner, the blazing air flooded the prodigious architecture with strange radiance, their blocks of emerald cemented by fire.

At the twelfth stroke, the flames sculpted atop the cupola on the summit of the dome came to life, stirred and fanned by the beating wings of the black bird.

All the doors of the mausolea opened...

Twelve

Our companions, who were now running out of breath, did not know how to get out of the plaza, which was surrounded by a series of identical exits. Polly Bird, mad with terror, was still crying: "Run! Go on! Make haste!" but did not think to give them the necessary directions. They ran around the fatal circle as fast as they could, already exhausted and breathless, unaware that they were no longer making progress and repeatedly treading the same circular course.

"By the Gate of the Bat!" Polly cried, finally. "The portal is through there! Run, by Heaven and Hell! Your lives are hanging by a thread!"

They immediately raced into one of the six great squares forming the rose–the one marked by a statue of a bat. The other four, of which we have not spoken, were dignified by a spider, a vulture, a cat and a leech. I should say that Ned Barton, and Grey Jack even more so, fervently desired to let go of the iron coffin, which slowed their progress, but how could they get out of that abominable labyrinth without it? No exit was perceptible.

Meanwhile, the crystal bell proceeded to sound its last strokes. Throughout the city, immobility gave way to movement, silence to noise. Through every open doorway, the interiors of the mausolea could be seen, their inhabitants rising from their shells and attending to their toilettes. Some of them had already appeared at their thresholds. The men of considerable stature, but for the most part effeminate; the females, by contrast, were both tall and bold.

All of them, males and females alike, were molded in a green material, marbled with dark red, with yellow shining eyes and lips which burned and sparkled, like coals in a forge excited by the bellows. Long purple veils flowed from their shoulders, and it was easy to see by the ever-more-intense glow which lit up the air that each of them had a bloody puncture on the left side of the breast, at which a ruby-red droplet quivered...

Were they not yet fully awake, or were our fugitives under some protection? None of these frightful creatures had yet perceived them, although nothing hid them from view. Polly Bird no longer dared call out within the coffin for fear of attracting their attention. Our Anna commended her soul to God, because she felt sure that her poor harassed limbs would carry her no further. Ned was not in good spirits; Grey Jack, although he was English to the core, was all gooseflesh; Merry Bones himself felt the pressure of time building.

"Courage!" whispered Polly Bird, who saw them falter. "One last effort! We are very close to the gate-keeper's tomb. To obtain passage, it will be sufficient to throw a little of the ash of my defunct seducer into his eyes. Courage!"

But at that instant the black bird, with its wings spread, alighted in the middle of the flames in the punchbowl which crowned the great dome and launched its last "cuckoo." The final chime of the crystal clock had sounded, and a distant cry was heard, followed by the sound of a hunting-horn.

Then, before another second had elapsed, the cries and trumpetings were doubled and redoubled with magical velocity, and our fugitives were surrounded by a vast clamor.

The voice of the hunting-horns sounded above all else. The shouts were formulated in an unknown language, and there are no words to describe the harrowing sonorousness of the fanfare sounded by the horns. At the same time, from the four points of the compass, invisible drums beat out a call to arms and the crystal bell sounded a tocsin.

"We are two steps from the doorway!" said Polly Bird. "They are crying: The Sepulchre is violated! A vampire is dead!–but we're there. One last surge, and we're out!"

It was true. Our fugitives could already see the high wall of porphyry, a marvel among marvels, girdling the low, deep and narrow arch that was the only entrance to the immense city. They must have passed through that arch on their arrival, although they had no memory of it at all–and as they had already passed the last of the mausolea, there was no one between them and the great gaping portal, beyond which was the night.

But the clamor–the fanfares, the call to arms and the tocsin, mingled with all kinds of noise–was swelling and rising like a tide.

The din was deafening, and an innumerable mob of men, women, four-legged animals, reptiles and birds suddenly hurled themselves into the street from every exit. They were uniformly clad in red and green, with yellow eyes, and they filled the street within the blink of an eye.

"Kill! Kill! Gatekeeper, close the portal! Drop the portcullis and lower the bridge! Loose the dogs, the lions, the tigers, the crocodiles, the serpents! The Sepulchre is violated! A vampire is dead! There must be blood, blood, blood!"

It was an astounding sight–but there was not the slightest response from beside the portal to the vociferations of the crowd. The gatekeeper did not show himself at all. The portcullis remained suspended and the drawbridge stayed down. No dogs could be seen, nor tigers, nor crocodiles, nor serpents.

With your permission, I shall take time out to explain this. Each of the inhabitants of Selene took a twenty-four hour turn at taking charge of the unique gate. Today was the day when that duty fell to Monsieur Goetzi–and because he had a reputation for punctuality, his predecessor had stood down at the first stroke of the twenty-fourth hour. He was wrong to do so, and I expect that he was punished for his negligence.

For this reason, our fugitives had no one to bar their retreat–but, great God, their position was hardly any less precarious! The furious and tumultuous tide of assailants was growing with increasing rapidity. They were already abreast of their quarry, to the right and the left, when the voice of the coffin cried: "Look out, Merry Bones! Protect yourself!"

The brave Irishman turned around, and the breath from the hugely gaping mouth of a hurrying green vampire burned his face, while two monstrous dogs leapt snapping at his throat and a swarm of hissing reptiles slid between his legs.

The moment was critical–all the more so because he was simultaneously beset from both sides by the yelping, croaking, baying, roaring crowd, crying: "Kill! Kill!"– and the fugitives, spurred on by the voice of the coffin, took the bit between their teeth.

Merry Bones paused for no more than a quarter of a second, but it was enough to separate him from the rest of his companions, who were passing through the arch and leaving him all alone in the city of Selene.

She would never have consented voluntarily to leave anyone–even an Irishman–at the mercy of such cruel enemies, but Polly urged them on like a maniac, knowing the fate that awaited her if she were recaptured–and we will soon see that she had ambitions of her own, in her capacity as the sole heir of Monsieur Goetzi. Edward Barton and Grey Jack, obedient to her voice, passed over the drawbridge and through the arch, running like hares.

Anna followed them without knowing that she was saved, or at least outside the evil city. *She* alone turned around on the far side of the moat, and was able to take one last look, through the opening of the arch, at the most magnificent and infernal spectacle that any group of mortals had ever seen since the beginning of time.

Intrepid as *She* was by nature, *She* certainly did not regret the dangerous hour *She* had spent among those fantastic terrors–but a great dizziness took hold of her thoughts. Following the instincts of her poetic temperament, *She* retained the impression of those miracles wrought by a power other than God's: the moment of awakening, when the sepulchral fairyland had recovered its orgiastically violent colors, left a particularly vivid memory, like a wound.

The hole pierced by the arch in the thick blackness of the rampart gave her one last glimpse of it: the orgy, bounding and rolling in an ocean of green and red light. And beyond the confused movements of the populace drunk with rage, *She* saw again, as if in an already distant dream, the infinite landscape of tombs, domes and colonnades lost in sparkling vestibules...

But *She* could not see any sign of poor Merry Bones, who was by then utterly drowned in the depths of the crowd.

"God be praised," *She* said. "We have been delivered from great peril."

"Forward! Forward!" replied Polly. "We are not yet in a position to congratulate ourselves. There will be time enough to thank God when we have passed out of the girdle of shadows and can see the bell-towers of Semlin before us!"

I hardly need to add that in passing through the arch, our companions had re-entered the darkness which surrounds Selene on every side, like an impenetrable suburb.

They resumed their march, and those among them who could not help thinking of Merry Bones were very careful not to mention his name.

We, on the other hand, will focus our attention upon him.

Thirteen

Merry Bones was both surprised and annoyed by the furious attack launched upon him by the vampires, because he had thought that they were still some way behind him. Such miscalculations are easy to make when in combat with unnatural creatures; their normal agility and litheness far exceeds that of humans. His astonishment did not, however, prevent him from planting his head in the stomach of the giant whose breath had burned him.

The impact filled the mattress of his hair with a coldness so disagreeable that he promised himself that, even though he was not proud, he would only use his feet on other beasts of the same kind. In spite of the beautiful appearance of jasper, the breast of the villainous giant was as flabby and ice-cold as the belly of a fish.

The head-butt had been solid, however, and the giant, having been hurled backwards into the crowd, did not fall over until he had knocked down half a dozen monsters. That gave Merry Bones a little room for maneuver, and enabled him to look behind him.

A howling, moving wall already separated him from his companions; he was cut off, surrounded and abandoned.

"Just like the English!" he said to himself, his opinion of the most civilized of nations unjustly lowered by his misfortune. "But perhaps they have enough good sense to understand that an Irishman can always look after himself!" And he set himself to launch a fusillade of kicks in every direction, so numerous and so powerful that the vampires saw stars by the million.

Unfortunately, there was no one to enjoy that amazing spectacle: a simple domestic servant, keeping at bay a riot composed of all the vampires on Earth, driven to the utmost extreme by their fury. It is highly improbable, I admit, but quite true–and Merry Bones, while beating them back, even sang snatches of Irish songs and hurled vile insults at them. Such was the pardonable produce of his poor education.

In all fairness, though, they were simply too many. They came on, and they kept coming. The dogs, especially, demonstrated their wrath; the birds came at him with intolerable relentlessness; and when the spiders and the fetid bats joined in the fray, Merry Bones lost patience. It is not that master vampires are so very numerous–happily, they are not, or the whole world would be exsanguinated–but apart from the fact that they have their own doubles, each one has in his train accessories which can also redouble themselves. Every vampire functions as a great finance house or a noble family, maintaining as many as a hundred clients or servants–and the members of the vampire aristocracy never have less than fifty. That gave the city of Selene a variable population, which could re-enter into itself like the elements of a telescope or the various parts of a fishing-rod. It was exhausting; within that abominable meadow, swarming with life and direly in need of a thorough mowing, nothing could be done.

We have arrived at a moment when poor Merry Bones was seriously embarrassed. He had two dogs at each leg, three spiders on his back, a bat within each armpit and several dozen leeches distributed hither and yon about his body. Four great vultures quarreled over his eyes–and all the while, the green men struck out at him vigorously with all manner of weapons. That bravest of servants was, in consequence, severely inconvenienced.

Suddenly, he clapped a hand to his forehead; an idea had occurred to him. He had placed the soup-ladle between his legs in order to have the free use of his arms. You will not have forgotten that it contained the ashes of the burned heart of Monsieur Goetzi. Merry Bones remembered that Polly had praised the virtue of those ashes very highly. Desirous of seeing something of what they could do, he dropped to his knees in order to cramp the style of the vermin that were harassing him, then flailed his fists so heroically that he forced his persecutors to retreat a pace or two.

Having thus made room, he took up the ladle and thrust it beneath the nose of the first green man to press forward upon him again.

The effect was most satisfactory. The green man immediately exploded. What could, I suppose, be called a sneeze had dislocated and fragmented him, clothing and all, causing considerable collateral damage around him.

This result afforded Merry Bones such a welcome surprise that his determination to live was renewed. He ran through every oath known in the west of Ireland and planted the handle of the ladle in his plaited hair, where it was as firmly held as a nail embedded in oak. He briskly executed the steps of an Irish jig to the imagined tune of Lilliburlero, then signaled that he wanted to talk.

"Do you gang of snakes understand the Irish?" he said. "If you want me to quiet down, I'll agree not to exterminate you all to the very last one, but if you continue to annoy me..."

He was interrupted by a piercing din of male voices, female yappings, canine howls, bird-cries, reptilian hisses and shrill bat-calls. The gist of the clamor was: "You are our prisoner. The gate is closed now, the port-cullis lowered, the bridge lifted. If we cannot defeat you by force, hunger will kill you and we shall feed your blood to our swine."

Poor Merry Bones was already beginning to feel the pangs of appetite. The thought of dying of starvation was parent to an entirely legitimate anger.

"We shall see about that, you hundred devils and more!" he cried, rolling up his sleeves. And, taking hold once again of his magic ladle, he marched resolutely towards the portal to the outside world.

No one impeded his passage. The mob kept its distance, laughing in a mocking fashion.

On arriving at the gate, poor Merry Bones found that it was indeed closed and barricaded. He tried to release it, but it would have been easier to shake the towers of Westminster Abbey. Disappointed by this mishap, he hesitated indecisively, and his embarrassment caused the rabble to laugh all the more heartily.

"He who laughs last laughs loudest!" snarled Merry Bones, who would have scratched his ears till they bled for a plan.

The riff-raff replied, from a distance: "You'll die of hunger, you dirty beggar! Hunger! Hunger!"

"Hunger! Hunger!" Merry Bones repeated, mimicking them—but in trying to mock them with a gesture popular among common folk, he was unfortunate enough to upset the soup-ladle and spill the ashes of Monsieur Goetzi's burnt heart upon the ground.

The vampires raise a howl of triumph to celebrate this accident, whose consequences were incalculable, and the horrible crowd shook with a new fury, Merry Bones could not help being a trifle disconcerted at first, but he patted his head three times and said with a broad Irish wink: "That's the idea! Let's see who'll be laughing now!"

The fallen ash had settled at the steel-lined foot of the closed door. While the tumultuous mob came forward again, Merry Bones scraped the ground, gathering as much of the powder as he could in his ladle and collecting the rest in a little heap.

The entire pack of bipeds, quadrupeds, birds and ophidians flung themselves upon him together. He picked out a fine hussy reeking of perfume and seized a handful of her blonde mane at the scruff of the neck. He did it so rapidly that no one could prevent him, and there was scarcely time for a curse to pass the virago's flaming lips. In spite of the bites, the stings and the blows of wing and bludgeon, Merry Bones' powerful arms bent her over until her mouth touched the little heap of ash.

You already have some idea of the violence produced by a vampire's encounter with the only substance capable of causing one to burst asunder. No sooner had the courtesan's lips of flame made contact with the ash when there was not merely an explosion but a veritable eruption, like that of Vesuvius or Etna. The steel-lined door was lifted from its hinges and thrown to an incredible distance; the portcullis shattered into a thousand pieces; the wall was reduced to a rubble which would have served as adequate filling for a road–and yet, by some curious fluke, the drawbridge itself remained intact, although its chains broke, allowing it to fall vertically to its usual place above the moat, as if for the express purpose of granting free passage to poor Merry Bones.

Do I need to tell you about the damage done to the mob? No–you can easily imagine it. It will suffice for you to know that Merry Bones suffered only a number of insignificant scratches, a few bruises and the scorching of a couple of outer layers of his woolly hair. He figured that he could easily get his hair cut the next day, and that what he had lost had not been worth saving.

"Nice trick, eh boys?" he said to the vampiral mincemeat that surrounded him. "Look after yourselves."

And he crossed the bridge, holding his sides to contain his laughter.

Despite his brilliant success, poor Merry Bones' troubles had not yet ended. Once the bridge was behind him, he was beset by deep, opaque and impenetrable night. He moved off immediately, striding out purposefully–but after several paces, surprised that he could not hear any noise, he turned around. He saw nothing.

The darkness was complete and the silence absolute. The only effect of his turning around was that Merry Bones lost his sense of direction, and he set off again at random, oppressed by terror of the unknown. He should have gone straight ahead, that much is certain, but the people of his country have weathervanes in their heads. Suddenly, without any apparent reason, he was seduced by a passing whim into turning right–and then, an instant afterwards, became convinced that he was heading back into Selene and turned left.

It is difficult to make progress in this fashion, and such was the case with poor Merry Bones, who hardly advanced at all. At the end of an hour, as he was changing direction for what was perhaps the twenty-first time, he collided with someone following a course at right-angles to his own.

"Blundering fool!"

"Ruffian!"

"Hey! Grey Jack!"

"Miss! Miss! That sluggard Merry Bones isn't dead!"

Following this exchange of words, a glimmer of light intruded upon the night and our Anna appeared, carrying a candle in her hand. It illuminated Ned, Jack and the iron coffin. They had lost Doctor Szegeli and the young Slavonian artist, minor characters whose eventual fate you will easily deduce when you know that the night was full of vengeful thirsty vampires who were looking for victims to devour.

Our Anna and her followers were lost, just like Merry Bones. Perhaps you are wondering how that came about, since they were accompanied by Polly Bird–who, as the former double of Monsieur Goetzi had become familiar with all manner of devilment. The reason is that the unfortunate Polly had fallen into a state of shock by virtue of the cutting of the mystical thread which bound her to her seducer and master. Such operations cannot be undergone without the general state of health suffering considerable effect. Subsequent events had been so terribly dramatic as to drain her strength. The air inside the iron coffin was not good, and the consequence of these combined circumstances was that the former Polly had fallen unconscious in her box, and all subsequent attempts to awaken her had been in vain.

A brief interval of rest allowed them to confer with one another. Merry Bones took advantage of this moment of leisure to free himself of numerous scraps of vampire flesh that were sticking to his hair and clothes. Our Anna examined this debris curiously, from the viewpoint of a natural historian. This was the outcome of her observations: *She* concluded that the density of

156

vampire flesh is rather tenuous; it is soft and a trifle sticky; by night a pale green phosphorescent glow diffuses therefrom into the shadows; by day, on the other hand, it is dark green, marbled with red and black. In science, there are no unimportant details–and I give you this information, moreover, for the same price that it cost me.

The unanimous decision of the conference was that they had to pierce that crust of darkness by any means possible. They guessed that it could not be later than two o'clock in the afternoon; consequently, once they arrived at the frontier of the false night, they would find themselves in broad daylight again.

Merry Bones took up his place at the head of the column once again, and ordered the departure. After a long and monotonous march, a cry of gladness escaped from every bosom: "Light!"

It was no more than a faint twilight, but their joy at perceiving it was hardly less than that which would have been occasioned by absolute clarity. Our friends quickened their paces–until they stopped abruptly, frozen by terror.

Shades of green had suddenly appeared in the atmosphere. At the same time, a dull noise–reminiscent of the reverberations generated by a troop of cavalry–became audible. Long threads of livid shadow were sliding about them to the left and right.

"The vampires! The vampires!"

It was only too true! All the inhabitants of Selene who were still able-bodied had saddled up their dogs, their lions and their tigers, and that monstrous cavalry had already surrounded our unfortunate companions. Meanwhile, other villains, mounted on bats of various species, arrived by air amid the clatter of membranous wings.

It was hopeless. Merry Bones had left his famous ladle behind–they were finished!

At the very moment of the utmost desperation, while the bloodthirsty cohort ranged itself on either side of our friends, celestial music was heard in the distance; and–need I say it?–the darkness recoiled before that enchanted harmony, which seemed to bring with it the beloved light of day.

The vampire horde, after an instant's astonishment and indecision, was sent howling in retreat, like a hundred demons put to flight by the approach of a single angel.

It was indeed an angel of sorts that was coming.

Like actual angels, such adorable beings only appear in order to work miracles. There is not even any need to think of them or wish for them: their blissful presence is sufficient.

The Right Honorable Arthur *** (the one whom we called, in another country, and with adequate reason, "the unknown comparable to a god") had not come to the plains of Serbia to protect Anna and her companions. As in Holland, previously, he was studying the art of warfare under the direction of the respectable member of the Anglican clergy who accompanied him in the role of tutor. He was here visiting the battlefields which had secured the fame, successively, of Suleiman II, the prince of Bavaria, Prince Eugene [22] and so many others.

Yes, it was the honorable Arthur–blond, rosy-cheeked and beardless–in his admirable comfortable carriage. While the venerable clergyman took his siesta after a substantial meal, the young lord, momentarily forgetful of his precocious labors, was singing "God Save the King" to the accompaniment of a guitar.

He passed by. He did not even see those whose lives he had saved.

Fourteen

Our Anna did not wish to return to Semlin. The company left the incontinent Danube and took a westerly direction in order to race, at last, to the assistance of the unhappy Cornelia.

Monsieur Goetzi was no longer to be feared, so the journey across the fertile but little-known fields of Bosnia–where the women dressed very becomingly–was perfectly agreeable. The Tina Pass provided a convenient way through its mountains. Once on the other side, they could see the haughty peaks of the Dinaric Alps, in whose bosom Castle Montefalcone nestled.

The iron coffin had now been empty for several days. Polly Bird's conduct while they had been in the city of Selene had been so admirable that there had been no opposition to setting her free. She had not abused the privilege. The immoderate use she made of alcoholic beverages whenever the occasion presented itself surprised no one, because English village girls have a taste for liquor, which is even shared by some young women of better birth. In any case, she wore male clothing, which made her frequent lapses into drunkenness seem less improper.

You will not have forgotten that she continued to play the role of Monsieur Goetzi's double, that being the only means that had to secure the passage of Edward S. Barton esquire, through the high walls of the inaccessible castle. Homer had employed a similar strategy in his immortal epic; the iron coffin would serve as a reduced version of the Trojan horse.

Physically, Polly had changed somewhat since the death of her seducer. She was diminished in every sense

160

of the word and presented the image of a Monsieur Goetzi reduced by fatigue or illness–but she had nevertheless retained a self-important manner which displeased our Anna. Merry Bones alone had the gift of her obedience. There was no mystery in this–he planted his head in her stomach or applied a foot to her backside every time she did not fall in with his plans.

The evening of the sixth day found them in the mountain gorges, and the moonlight soon illuminated the imposing mass of the noble dwelling which *She* so famously described under the name of the *Castle of Udolpho*.

No lights shone on its ramparts, nor in the gothic windows of the main building. The ancient fortress would have seemed entirely dead had not a human form been visible at the top of the highest tower: a young woman clad in long white veils–or her shade.

"Look there! I know her!" said our Anna

And Ned, wringing his hands with emotion, cried: "O Cornelia, my bride! Is it you that I see, or only your beloved ghost?"

In order to bring their enterprise to a successful conclusion, our companions had to separate into two groups. Monsieur Goetzi, as we shall now call the unfortunate Polly Bird, would enter the castle alone with the iron coffin; this would be carried by two local men hired in the town of Bihacz, about which the waters of the river Una divide. Our Anna, Merry Bones and Grey Jack would remain on watch outside.

The moment of parting was cruel. Long voyages engender intimacy, and facing common dangers creates a strong sense of togetherness–and I have not hidden from you the fact that *She* had previously honored Edward S. Barton with the first sympathetic impulse of her innocent heart. When he left her–perhaps forever–*She* shed a few tears; soon enough, however, the exceptional vigor of her character took over and *She* said in a firm tone: "Go, Edward Barton, my brother and my friend, as I am obliged to call you. Be as prudent as you are brave in the midst of the unknown perils that will surround you. Remember that my best wishes go with you, and that I am ready, night and day, to fly to your aid."

She turned around and the iron coffin was opened. Edward Barton lay down inside it; the two men from Bihacz placed it on their hand-barrow.

Monsieur Goetzi, naturally, had the password. As soon as he had shouted across the moat–having no horn on him–and given the necessary signal to the sentry, he was allowed to approach. When he was asked what he wanted, he replied: "To see Count Tiberio, immediately."

"The Count is taking his evening meal," came the reply, "and this is not a good time to see him."

"Any time is good for the delivery of good news," Monsieur Goetzi riposted. "Go find the Count and tell him that the man who has arrived carries the iron coffin."

The servant obeyed. Monsieur Goetzi, left alone with Edward, crouched down to one of the holes and whispered: "All is going marvelously. Sleep–pretend that you are quite dead."

"I am fully determined to save my bride," Ned replied, "but it is stifling in here, on my honor!"

The return of the servant put an end to the conversation.

The Count was waiting for Monsieur Goetzi in his apartment. The hired men replaced the coffin on their stretcher, carrying it along numerous corridors, past several dozen rooms which would have been magnificent had their dilapidation not testified to their centuries-long abandonment. Monsieur Goetzi could not repress an infernal smile as they passed the remains which marked the former bedroom of the Dowager Countess of Montefalcone.

That entire part of the castle, now fallen into disrepair, reminded him of the expedition undertaken by his defunct patron, and he said to himself: "That was well done–but I shall do better!" You have already guessed, I suppose, that the confidence of poor Ned and our Anna had been terribly misplaced.

They arrived at last in a better kept area, where the wall-hangings had been mended and the furniture dusted. Count Tiberio Palma d'Istria was sitting–or, rather, wallowing–in an enormous armchair whose form was reminiscent of those used by the Doges. He was drunk, as he usually was nowadays after dinner. Letizia had cultivated his bestial habits in order to enhance her dominion over him.

Monsieur Goetzi entered, followed by his two porters, who deposited the iron coffin on the tiled floor. They were ordered to leave, but made no move to withdraw.

"Good evening, you old scoundrel," said Tiberio. "Is that the Englishman that you have brought us in the box?"

"Greetings, my lord," said Monsieur Goetzi. "Yes, it's the Englishman."

"Is he quite dead?"

"I am astonished that you are not already inconvenienced by the odor of the corpse."

Tiberio immediately pinched his nose, trustingly.

"Would you like to see him?" asked Monsieur Goetzi, turning towards the coffin.

"Certainly not!" the Count exclaimed. "I've just eaten; it wouldn't be good for my digestion. The Englishman must be worm-food by now, for you've certainly taken your time bringing him here, old fellow."

"He was heavy, and the road was long," Monsieur Goetzi replied.

"It's quite a stink! Let's get on with it. What did I promise you for your reward?"

"Signora Letizia Pallanti."

"Is that right, you old scoundrel? That's marvelous. I loved her like the apple of my eye, but everything passes, and she wears the wig of a dead woman. Oh, poor Countess Greete. That was a good joke! Now, I have a fancy to marry Cornelia, my pupil, so that I might possess her youth as well as her fortune... oh well, throw the Englishman into the oubliette. I give you Letizia– now go away. Tell them as you go to open another bottle and bring my pupil Cornelia to me."

Thereupon, Monsieur Goetzi left with the iron coffin, and Count Tiberio resumed drinking. Edward Barton, in spite of the discomfort of his situation, congratulated himself on the success of the ruse. He thought that he was now being taken to Cornelia, and that she would easily find a means of letting his friends into the castle. That had been the plan, and Ned's hope was strengthened by the fact that Monsieur Goetzi did not carry out Count Tiberio's orders to the letter. He relayed the command to open another bottle of wine but did not mention Cornelia at all.

How many corridors, drawbridges, staircases, hallways and occupied rooms were there between Tiberio's apartment and Letizia's? The beautiful Italian was lying in the Oriental fashion upon a pile of cushions. She had grown very plump of late. It was here that our dear Edward S. Barton obtained a better understanding of his situation!

"Have you brought him to me alive?" cried *la Pallanti*, as soon as she saw Monsieur Goetzi–and when he had replied in the affirmative, she lifted herself up from her cushions and cried: "O Heaven! How wretched the darling love must be in there! Open the box at once, so that I may clasp him to my heart and intoxicate myself with the sight of him!"

Monsieur Goetzi, however, demurred. "Gently! The young man is robust and resolute. If we set him free, he will make us regret it."

"Do you think," Letizia asked, "that he is strong enough to resist my charms?"

"I am sure of it. Have you forgotten that he is in love with Cornelia?"

"That sparrow!" she exclaimed, shrugging her capacious shoulders. "I'll wager she carries no more than a hundred pounds of good flesh!"

Monsieur Goetzi made a face and replied: "You can say that again. Such that she is, however, she is all the recompense I seek."

Ned thought that he had misunderstood. "Perhaps, after all, Polly is making a joke," he thought.

"It's a fair price," said the Italian woman, however. "I promised her to you and you shall have her, but not right away."

"Why wait? I'm in a hurry."

"Because we must first get rid of that imbecile Tiberio."

"That will take time," Monsieur Goetzi objected.

"It will be all over by tomorrow morning," Letizia replied. "If you're thirsty, ask for my eleventh chambermaid: sixteen years old, a rosebud! I took her from the farm this morning and you will find her blood fresher by far than Cornelia's."

Monsieur Goetzi's eyes sparkled. Edward saw it through one of the little holes. The scales fell from his eyes. He realized with horror that Polly was still a vampire and that he was in her hands.

"I shall not refuse the little peasant," Monsieur Goetzi replied, "for I have had a good deal of trouble during my journey and few opportunities to obtain a good meal—but I warn you that you must not have a false sense of security. You have enemies outside the castle."

"What enemies?"

"Miss Anna Ward and her servants."

Ned shivered between the encasing walls, but he had sufficient spiritual fortitude not to betray his displeasure by any intemperate exclamation. There was an interval of silence, however, between the Italian woman and Monsieur Goetzi. She seemed to be thinking deeply.

"Listen," she said, at last. "You must go along the subterranean passage to the north; it is the shortest of four, only mile long. When you come to the end, you have only to turn a rock mounted on a pivot and you will find yourself in open country. Diligently make your way back to the Englishwoman and her men and offer to take them to Cornelia immediately. Bring them to me, and I'll take care of the rest. You've heard me—now do as I say. In the meantime, I shall furnish my beautiful Edward with explanations, after which he will give me his heart and his hand with pleasure."

Our Cornelia's prison was on the topmost floor of the tower. It was not out of pity but because he feared that her beauty would be affected by excessive seclusion that Count Tiberio had allowed her to take her exercise on the roof-platform. There, in that narrow enclosure, surrounded by battlements, she dwelt alone with thoughts of her young lover and regrets of happiness fled. The vast panorama of nature elevated her soul while nourishing her melancholy. The prodigious vault of the sky which loomed over her–a splendid cupola of blue by day, a million diamonds suspended in its depths by night–banished her despair by relating it to God. This was the white apparition that our friends had perceived as they arrived at the foot of the mountain.

That evening, tired of contemplating the sky, she lowered her gaze to the earth and was startled to observe a fire on the neighboring mountainside. She had never seen anything like it before. Full of astonishment–and perhaps, already, of hope–she fixed upon that glimmer with all the strength of her young eyes, afraid that she might be dreaming. She thought she recognized Anna, her best friend; Grey Jack, the old servant at the cottage; and Merry Bones, her dear Edward's valet. A fourth person was standing before the fire, but while his back was turned, his face could not be seen. Perhaps it was Edward! It ought to be Edward!

"Edward! Edward!" she cried, with an unutterable surge of joy.

Alas, he whom she had taken for Edward was Monsieur Goetzi, who had rejoined his friends by means of the northern underground passage–and who, following his deceptive scheme, was attempting to lead them to their destruction.

Following the departure of Monsieur Goetzi, Edward S. Barton was alone with Signora Letizia. That cunning woman was now showing him evidence of the most tender amiability.

"Dear boy," she said to him in a soft voice, "do you not see that everything that has happened is the result of my love for you? It began at the time when, having set aside your studies, you came to spend your vacations at the cottage I was visiting with my student, Cornelia de Witt, who has me to thank for her brilliant education. I cannot look at you now, your lip shadowed by light down and dressed with all the charms of adolescence, without a flutter in my frail heart. Having been brought up to observe the strictest standards, I had every respect for convention, but I promised myself that I would put the prodigious talents God gave me to good use in recovering the fortune of my forefathers in order that I might one day be worthy to unite my destiny with yours."

Edward S. Barton was an Englishman, so he had spirit. Despite the utter horror which this kind of discourse inspired in him, he resolved to counter it with equally skillful trickery.

"In the embarrassing situation in which I find myself," he replied, in an insinuating tone, "it is very difficult, Madame, to entertain thoughts of love. The walls of this coffin prevent the uplift of my heart–and how can I yield to your charms when I do not have the pleasure of seeing them?"

Letizia reflected for a moment, struck by the justice of this observation.

"I agree that we would be more comfortable," she said, finally, "if you and I could exchange words of love while accommodated upon my cushions–but prudence forbids it. Anyhow, in modern times, marriage is not altogether a matter of sentiment; I ought to open your eyes first. You have believed up to this point that that little girl, Cornelia de Witt, was rich and that I was poor. Abandon that error. Cornelia has nothing, and I am a rich heiress. Know that I am of royal blood. I have a vague memory of my cradle, richly ornamented with lace sewn with strings of fine pearls. A woman, beautiful as the day, bent over me as I slept, watching for my first smile. It was my mother! And my mother was named Princess Loiska Palma d'Istria, the elder sister-in-law of Count Tiberio."

It made no difference to Edward, but in the interests of making himself agreeable, he exclaimed: "Can it be possible!"

"I have the documents to prove it," Signora Letizia replied, "legitimated and registered. Shall I tell you how a company of Bohemians who prowled around the castle stole me away from the kisses of the princess, my mother...?"

"I'm so thirsty," Edward interrupted–but, as astute as she was shameless, Letizia took a glass from her bedside table, which she filled with excellent wine, and a straw. Having inserted the straw into one of the holes in the coffin and submerged the other end in the glass, she said: "Drink as much as you desire, dearest. I am happy to satisfy my beloved's least desire."

When he had drunk his fill, she continued. "Shall I tell you about the futile efforts my parents made to recover their only daughter? Unfortunately, their inquiries directed them to the Bohemian coast! Now, on the day that the wretches who had taken me had been approaching the coast, they were overwhelmed by Liparian corsairs, and I had fallen prey to the conquerors. I was five years old, my honor was intact. Algerian pirates took me from the corsairs, and I was prepared for the seraglio. A young eunuch helped me to escape and I returned to Italy, but I did not know the name and address of my parents. By turns a boarder in the most celebrated educational establishment in Turin, laureate of the Academy of Cracked Pots [23], fugitive, seller of antique earthenware potsherds to the English, reader to a cardinal, servant of one of the oldest eremites in the Apennines and assistant in the company of the famous bandit chief Rinaldo, I cannot believe that there was ever a youth so accident-prone as mine. This brought me to my fifteenth year. At that time, I found a man in rags dying in a thick wood. On seeing me, he gave a feeble cry and begged me to remove the shoe from my left foot. The requests of a man on the point of death are sacrosanct, so I obeyed, and he cried: 'It is she! God has granted that I can expiate the worst of my sins before I expire. You have a birthmark on the side of your foot beneath your ankle, young stranger. I recognize it, because it was I who snatched you from your cradle!' He then told me the name of my noble parents. I forgave him and he died in my arms. From that day forward, amid vicissitudes diverse and innumerable, my primary objective was to find my papers. My father had died of old age, laden with honors, and my mother had joined the saints in Heaven. Monsieur Goetzi, a dangerous but clever man whom I believed to be secretly a vampire, was very useful to me during my research. I encountered him at court. It was he who recommended me to take charge of the education of Cornelia, to bring me close to my uncle Count Tiberio–who desires, vainly now, to dispute with me the patrimony of Montefalcone–and it was I who placed Monsieur Goetzi close to you, so that he could teach you to esteem and cherish me."

"A nice gift!" said Edward.

"Judge me not!" the Italian woman pronounced, severely. "Love is my excuse. As for my pupil Cornelia de Witt, she's a conceited and ridiculous little fool, who has none but the beauty of the devil. She is not entitled to a penny of the heritage of the Counts of Montefalcone, I tell you. I shall take it all, as is my right, and the first use I shall make of my wealth will be to cover you in gold. Those are my terms. You are, of course, perfectly at liberty to reject my advances–but in either case, Miss Cornelia will be delivered to Monsieur Goetzi, who will drink her like a glass of lemonade."

Fifteen

We left Cornelia at the top of the tower in which she was held captive, watching from afar the fire beside which her friends were in conference with a stranger–who, seen from behind, she had taken for Edward. You know that this stranger was the former Polly Bird, who had now fully usurped the personality of Monsieur Goetzi.

I ought to tell you something of the plans formulated by that creature, lost by virtue of her close acquaintance with a monster. In spite of her native sex, she had resolved to marry Cornelia, by consent or by force, in order to possess the immense inheritance of the Counts of Montefalcone and attain noble status.

The pretended Monsieur Goetzi had just informed our Anna that he had completed his mission successfully and that Ned was safely installed in the heart of the enemy castle, but that he would need help to bring the adventure to a conclusion. Grey Jack and Merry Bones himself were taken in. During the expedition to the city of Selene, Polly Bird had given such a convincing demonstration of her loyalty they did not think to suspect her now.

Monsieur Goetzi, therefore, set himself at the head of the little troop, and guided them towards the mouth of the tunnel.

"Gather your courage," said the impostor, as he preceded our friends into the bowels of the earth. "A terrible night lies ahead of us."

Monsieur Goetzi had brought several torches made of resinous wood, which were lit–but their brightness was immediately swallowed up in the profound shadows of the cavern, only serving to illuminate a number of reptiles fleeing into the darkness here and there. In that darkness, a strange sound was born and died, rendering up a monstrous sigh.

"What's that?" asked our Anna, stopped in her tracks by a suffocating weight which oppressed her bosom.

"Go on," replied Monsieur Goetzi. "It's only Countess Elvina's old Aeolian harps, which went out of fashion and were put down here because there was no room in the attic."

She would have liked to ask more questions about this Countess Elvina, but Monsieur Goetzi was pressing on.

"Lift the torches!" Monsieur Goetzi instructed.

The order was obeyed, and the seeping walls of a vast subterranean chamber became vaguely discernible.

"Look up above your heads!" commanded Monsieur Goetzi, again.

They lifted their eyes. A high vault loomed above them, a huge round black hole at its center.

"What's that hole for?" asked our Anna.

"It's the entrance to Count Tiberio's oubliette," Monsieur Goetzi replied. "The victims fall through it into the pit–which you will find, if you care to look, directly beneath the hole."

"What?" cried our Anna, deeply offended. "Do such barbaric curiosities of the Middle Ages still exist? Has not the vivid enlightenment of philosophy annihilated all such horrors?"

Monsieur Goetzi gave a mocking laugh. "They are only too well remembered," he replied, "but I do not believe that anyone has made use of them since Countess Elvina."

She suddenly found herself in a Gothic hall of the most lugubrious aspect. Mounted on its tall fireplace was a Venetian mirror embossed with a representation of the passion of Our Lord. On the wall to the right of the fireplace, a white spot was visible amid the hangings of dark brown Cordovan leather: an ivory button. Monsieur Goetzi had a fat black cat in his arms, whose four feet he broke, one by one, with cold cruelty. "That's so he won't run away," he said. "You shall see something of its function. I shall put him in the same place as Countess Elvina. Watch the pussycat closely."

He placed the black cat–which was mewing pitiably–on a flooring-slab that was larger than its neighbors. The animal tried to move away, but could not do so by virtue of its broken feet. Monsieur Goetzi, laughing, walked to the wall where the ivory button was. He pushed the button with his finger; the slab swung down and the cat disappeared. Then the door opened, and Count Tiberio's henchmen came in, armed to the teeth.

Monsieur Goetzi pointed his finger at our Anna and her companions, saying: "Here they are–I deliver them to you."

This time, Merry Bones was powerless to resist; our unfortunate friends were put in chains and taken away...

You must now imagine a frightful dungeon, in whose depths our Anna is lying on some bits of straw, with a ring of iron around her neck. This was where her generous devotion had brought her!

"Young maid of Albion," said a gentle voice beside her, all of a sudden, "I am Countess Elvina de Montefalcone."

She raised her eyelids, which had been sealed by tears, and saw a pale woman kneeling beside her pallet.

The woman was still young, although suffering had turned her hair white.

"What!" our Anna exclaimed. "Is it possible that you have escaped the perils of the pit?"

"That happened several centuries ago," replied the pale woman, with a melancholy but pleasant smile. "We must concern ourselves with the present now. I have come into your dungeon at the behest of a particular power, and it will be my pleasure to break your chains forthwith. Get up. Freedom is granted to you."

She read in our Anna's expression an ardent desire for a more detailed explanation, and she obliged, continuing: "A barbarous usurper has condemned you to death. The one you call Monsieur Goetzi–who is none other than the infamous Gertrude de Pfafferchoffen, my rival, whose soul has passed after several other incarnations into the body of the village girl Polly Bird–has sold you. Do you know that Count Tiberio and Signora Letizia, separated for a while by covetousness and concupiscence, are reconciled tonight? Why? Because the young midshipman Barton has utterly repulsed the unseemly advances of the Italian woman, and the beautiful Cornelia has humiliated Count Tiberio with her disdain. Reunited by a common desire for vengeance, the two monsters with human faces are resolved to put Monsieur Barton and Mademoiselle de Witt to death this very night."

"How can I save them?" asked our Anna, wringing her hands.

"God is great," replied the pale woman, "and you are free!"

Our Anna threw herself towards the door of her dungeon, which opened before her as if by magic.

She marched forward, sustained by an instinctive hope. At the end of the seventh corridor, she encountered a stonemason who was sculpting a pair of arms in a block of alabaster. The two arms seemed to belong to two bodies of different sexes, and their hands were joined in an affectionate clasp.

The sculptor, desirous of embracing our Anna, said to her: "How do you like my work, my beauty? It's a pleasant whim of the gross Letizia, who wants it to ornament the tombs of the young Englishwoman and Cornelia."

She fled in desperation, while the laughing sculptor continued his work. By her count, she must have run for several leagues through corridors without end and derelict rooms.

Finally, in the corner of a gallery, *She* perceived a light under a door–and at the same time, her ears caught the sound of voices, some angry and others plaintive. *She* gathered her strength, which had been depleted by fatigue. *She* opened the door and entered, releasing a cry of terror at the sight of her two friends, Edward S. Barton and Cornelia, in chains.

Cornelia's beautiful hair had been cut short; Ned had a rope about his neck. They now wore the characteristic costume of those unfortunates tortured to death by the Inquisition in former times.

Behind them was a man of ferocious aspect entirely costumed in red. The axe that he carried on his shoulder was sufficient proof that his profession was that of executioner.

In another part of the room, a second group was formed by Count Tiberio, Signora Letizia and Monsieur Goetzi. The last-named, obviously discontented, was claiming that he had been promised that Cornelia would be delivered up to his unnatural thirst, while Letizia was making fun of him and Tiberio was threatening to have his head cut off. They were all raising and lowering their arms excitedly, like the roguish knaves they were.

At the sight of our Anna, they smiled cruelly.

"Just look at the bluestocking!" said the signora.

But *She*, heedless of this remark, fell upon her friends and clasped them in her arms.

"What good timing!" said the atrocious Italian. "Of her own accord, she takes up the position in which we can kill three birds with a single stone!" She turned round to take a step toward the fireplace, and the movement revealed the part of the wall that had been behind her. That favored our Anna with a shaft of sinister enlightenment. In her distress, she had not previously recognized the chamber above the oubliette; now, she saw the embossed Venetian mirror, the Cordovan leather hangings, and the ivory button.

"We must fly!" she exclaimed, in bewilderment.

It was too late. The Italian woman touched the button and the slab swung away–but our Anna, Cornelia and Ned were miraculously held above the drop by a supernatural hand.

Countess Elvina, emerging unexpectedly from the gulf, cried out with the voice of Mrs. Ward: "Now then dear, what's all this? Eyes open! Do you intend to lie abed till ten o'clock on your wedding day?"

There was a loud noise in the corridor. William Radcliffe blew his nose; Mr. Ward told him to go look for a locksmith.

"Save them" Save them!" cried our Anna, who found herself on her feet, in her wedding dress, in the middle of her room, with the March sun steaming joyously through the windows...

Epilogue

It seems that Milady made the error of smiling, for Miss 97 stopped abruptly.

"I take your meaning," she said, in a scandalized tone. "You think that our story will be concluded by that threadbare formula: It was a dream! Admit it! Well, that's where you're mistaken!"

She briskly drained the dregs of her last cup of tea and continued. "No, no, no, no! I would not trouble the gentleman for so little. *It was not a dream* [24]. In the first place, *She* had been subject to fits of 'second sight' since the age of nine, and her parents had taken care to conceal that gift or infirmity. Be assured that I do not mean to say that *She* had accomplished so long and so eventful a journey in a single night—but there are other things than dreams, as you will see. When *She* finally opened her door, Mr. Radcliffe and her parents were awestruck by the change which had overtaken her person. *She* looked at them distractedly and demanded to know what had become of Countess Elvina. They thought her mad, all the more so when *She* extracted a formal promise that as soon as the marriage was over, they would depart for Montefalcone, with the stipulation that they would go via Rotterdam.

"And immediately after the ceremony, they left, for she held to the bargain. I remind you of the letters received the previous evening; those letters were certainly not a dream, and they had offered a glimpse of what had become of Ned and Cornelia.

"Henceforth, I shall only give you the facts without imposing any interpretation on them. When they arrived in London, the first thing that struck our Anna's eyes was a poster thus inscribed:

MAIN ATTRACTION!!!
THE DEVOURING OF A YOUNG VIRGIN
BY THE AUTHENTIC VAMPIRE
OF PETERWARDEIN
WHO WILL DRINK SEVERAL PINTS OF BLOOD
AS IS HIS HABIT
WITH THE MUSIC OF THE HORSEGUARDS
WONDERFUL ATTRACTION INDEED!!!

"*She* pointed out that poster to Grey Jack, but the old and faithful servant had no memory of it. The phenomenon which had served as the basis of this story was absolutely personal to our Anna.

"They crossed the channel. On disembarking at Rotterdam, *She* relocated the broken road where the young unknown comparable to a god had offered his regards to her for the first time.

"*She* stayed the night at the *Ale and Amity*, in the room with the stovepipe hole, the floral curtains and the battles of Admiral Ruyter. *She* recognized everything, down to the minutest detail."

"And the city of Selene?" asked Milady.

"Wait—let me tell it. They went immediately, as fast as possible, to Montefalcone, where they arrived on the day of Corny and Ned's wedding."

"Saved by Countess Elvina, I hope?" the terrible countess interrupted again.

"No," replied Miss 97, with a hint of embarrassment, "but there really was a local legend concerning that unfortunate victim of feudalism. Count Tiberio and Letizia undoubtedly nurtured the most perfidious designs against the affianced couple; that they did not dare to execute their plans was due to an intervention which I do not hesitate to describe as providential. The young Lord Arthur *** came to the locality, accompanied by his tutor, the respectable clergyman, to study at first hand the famous battlefield of Scanderbeg [25]...”

“And that was sufficient to frustrate the plots of the two villains?” Milady exclaimed.

“Yes, Madame,” replied Miss Jebb dryly. “If I could only tell you the glorious, almost divine, name of that young nobleman...”

“And Monsieur Goetzi?”

“He had married the widow of a tradesman.”

“But Selene! Selene, the dead city!”

“Certain things, Milady,” replied Miss Jebb, gravely, “remain beyond our understanding, and even of that which you possess by virtue of your nobility. One must have the protection of a vampire to enter Selene, and there is not always one at hand. Our two newly-married couples went to Semlin with Grey Jack and Merry Bones–whose shaggy hair really was diminished by three quarters–-and although they could not find Selene, they found the shopkeepers who had sold the stove, the charcoal and the iron ladle. There is, in addition, the fact that the disappearance of the surgeon Magnus Szegeli was notorious in the town, and the home of the Slavonian sketch-artist had been empty for three weeks.”

At his point, Miss 97 got up, and made her final bow.

A few days ago, in Paris, I received the following letter from the county of Stafford:

Dear Sir,

She *had the habit of adding justificatory and explanatory comments to the conclusions of her compositions. Everything is clear in our story except for that* which concerns the young unknown comparable to a god.

I think that it would be as well to lift the veil; your book will thus gain in historical importance. This could be done by adding a postscript in which you would say:

"We have not dared to inscribe in these frivolous pages a name which filled the world with its incomparable brilliance: the name of he who put Napoleon Bonaparte in his pocket, and who surpasses other modern heroes as far as Achilles did his Greek and Trojan rivals, etc, etc"–a deft allusion to the statue which the nuns of Lourdes erected to His Grace, in a Greek costume which might be reckoned a little too high above the knee by common folk.

Or it could be a simple note, heavily underscored and worded as follows: IT WAS WELLINGTON!!! (with several exclamation points).

I, for my part, would prefer the latter expedient.

Yours truly, etc.

JEBB.

Afterword

Although *Vampire City* was considered in its own day–
even by its author–to be a relatively minor work, it is
likely to seem far more interesting to modern readers and
historians than many of Féval's other productions. It is
the most innovative and extravagant of the three novels
which employ the motif of the vampire, and now that
vampire fiction has become a genre of its own, its enterprise and historical significance are much more clearly
evident.

In the introduction to *Knightshade*, I argued that
Féval was also an important pioneer of what Robert
Scholes calls "metafiction"–defined as "experimental
fabulation" with reference to literary works whose acute
consciousness of their own fictitiousness involves the
explicit redeployment of material from other texts, usually in order to identify and investigate their tacit sub-
texts–and *Vampire City* carries that exploratory process
further to a greater extent than anything else Féval wrote
after 1860. For both these reasons, it can now be seen to
have been far ahead of its own time–a very modern book
whose modernity was quite imperceptible in 1867.

It is also a very odd book–I mean that as a compliment, of course–whose oddness has been further empha-
sized by intervening circumstance. When it was written,

there was no "stereotyped image" of the vampire, and writers were free to improvise as they wished.

In the afterword to *The Vampire Countess*, I pointed out that although the French tradition of popular vampire fiction began with pastiches of John Polidori's *The Vampyre*, its French adapters left out the tiny detail that was more garishly reproduced in *Varney the Vampyre*: the notion that vampiric predation involves neck-biting. There was not the slightest reason why Féval should feel obliged, in featuring vampires, to make them feed by biting their victims' necks, and the fact that the substitute methods he employs are very different–that of the ghoul Addhema does not even involve blood-drinking– only seems to us to be perverse because we are looking back from a post-Stokerian era. (Even Bram Stoker's emphasis on neck-bites would not seem so heavy were it not for the contribution made by innumerable movies in which paired punctures–impossibly spaced and incorrectly placed–have served as an iconic visual symbol of vampiric victimization.)

Although it is calculatedly bizarre in its own right, therefore, *Vampire City* seems even more bizarre when its imagery is seen in the shadow of Stoker's. Improbable as it may seem at first glance, however, the similarities between the development of the vampire motif in *Vampire City* and *Dracula* may be more significant than the differences, just as the difference between *Vampire City* and *The Vampire Countess* are more significant than the similarities.

Some of the background elements in *Vampire City*, including the setting, are carried forward from *The Vampire Countess*, emphasizing the continuity between the two works, but Monsieur Otto Goetzi and the Countess Addhema are very different characters. It is not at all certain that Addhema actually exists, or whether she is merely a myth cleverly deployed by the pseudonymous Countess Marcian Gregoryi in order to conceal her criminal activities–so cleverly that her three principal adversaries each suffer a crucial hallucination in which they see Addhema at work in all her supernatural glory. If the Countess really is Addhema, though, she is the ultimate *femme fatale*, mirroring the vision experienced by the viewpoint character of Charles Baudelaire's poem *Les Métamorphoses de la Vampire* (1857; tr. as *Metamorphoses of the Vampire*). The sexual element of her predation is not, however, confined to innocent young men like the novice priest in Théophile Gautier's *La Morte Amoureuse* (1836; tr. as *The Dead in Love*)–it embraces female victims as well as male, with a distinct preference for the very young; rather than drinking their blood as the means to the end of her own renewal, Addhema usurps their youth in a far more spectacular fashion, by ripping off their scalps and wearing their lustrous hair as a trophy of her success.

Although the entire story of which Monsieur Goetzi features may be a mythical invention–a figment of Ann Radcliffe's visionary experience–he is unambiguously real within that story. He is a multiple personality (and how!) but his multiplicity is very different from Countess Marcian Gregoryi's. Like Addhema, he does get involved in a hair-transplant, but his abilities are so mundane that he must do the job one hair at a time, and he does not renew himself in the process–he is merely a middleman between his employer and a fellow employee. He is not an aristocrat (although the point is made that he is one of the least of vampirekind, most of his rivals being far more powerful) and he is not sexy (although his ability to "dividuate" seemingly gives him an opportunity to commandeer sexy manifestations that he does not significantly exploit.

Unlike the Countess Addhema and Ange Ténèbre, the vampire from *Knightshade*, Monsieur Goetzi does not seem to regard vampiric predation as a matter of mere necessity or unavoidable temptation, partially eclipsed by a much more all-consuming desire for vast wealth; his interest in money seems to be the secondary consideration, and he is quite prepared to live as a virtual servant if that facilitates the discreet service of his appetite. This modification of the image of the vampire represents a considerable evolution–and Féval is very exceptional in having contrived such an evolution, because almost all the other authors who have written more than one vampire story have carried forward exactly the same image, if not the same character.

The text of *Vampire City* cannot, of course, refer back to the events of *The Vampire Countess*, which was set at a later date. What it can and does refer back to is the fictitious text cited and summarized within the earlier story: *La Légende de la Goule Addhema et du Vampire Szandor* by Hans Spurzheim, allegedly published in Bade in 1736. Féval almost certainly invented this "source;" as I recorded in the notes to *The Vampire Countess*, there is no French edition of any such book and I can find no trace of a German original, nor of any Spurzheim other than the phrenologist Johann Gaspar Spurzheim [26], who flourished at a slightly later date. There can be little doubt as to where Féval really obtained the information about folkloristic vampires which he transformed to suit his own purposes in *The Vampire Countess* and extrapolated into absurdity in *Vampire City*. It must have come from *Dissertations sur les Ap-*

paritions des Esprits, et sur les Vampires (1746) by Dom Augustin Calmet, a respected French Biblical scholar.

The evidence that Féval was borrowing from Calmet is clear in the text of *Vampire City*. Féval places Semlin in the *bannat de Temesvar*, the banate of Timisoara–a phrase used by Calmet to describe an allegedly vampire-infested region–and he also makes reference to the Tina Pass, another relatively obscure location mentioned by Calmet. Calmet makes much of the official report prepared by officers sent to investigate the case of the alleged vampire Arnold Paole, which had become something of a bestseller in the 1730s and had undoubtedly inspired his own treatise; his (unsupported) allegation that several unnamed German physicians had written accounts of similar cases presumably encouraged Féval to invent one. Calmet also uses the word oupire, although he makes no distinction between oupires and vampires (the confusion of vampires and ghouls, as noted in the afterword to *The Vampire Countess*, was first contrived by the German writer E.T.A. Hoffmann).

Calmet was also one of Bram Stoker's sources, and their common dependence on his work is the principal reason for the similarities between Féval's vampire stories and *Dracula*–but Stoker certainly never read Féval, and so his equally-extravagant embellishments of his source-material took him in a very different direction. We are nowadays so used to the Dracula-based image of the vampire that it is easy to forget that it was almost entirely Stoker's invention. There are elements borrowed from Calmet–the *Dissertations* had been partially translated into English as *The Phantom World*, published by Richard Bentley in 1850–but his other main source of inspiration (apart from his own nightmares) was his fellow graduate of Trinity College Dublin, Joseph Sheridan le Fanu, whose *Carmilla* (1872) was the best 19th-century vampire story written in English. Like *The Vampire Countess*, *Carmilla* is an intensely perverse *femme fatale* story, but it seems improbable that there was any direct influence. Again, Calmet was a common source, and le Fanu had probably read both Hoffmann's ghoul story and Gautier's *La Morte Amoureuse*, so the similarities between the methods by which Count Szandor and Carmilla–and, eventually, Lucy Westenra and Count Dracula–are destroyed are not particularly surprising, even though there is no precedent for them in Polidori or the works directly inspired by *The Vampyre*. There are, however some less obvious similarities between *Vampire City* and *Dracula* which are more interestingly co-incidental.

Stoker's vampires are frankly supernatural creatures which can only operate in darkness, being forced to remain comatose by day, bedded down on the soil of their homeland in coffin-like boxes. They are closely associated with bats and wolves, and are able to undergo remarkable metamorphoses, but they are allergic to garlic and recoil from symbols of Christian virtue. Their victims become vampires themselves.

These properties are haphazard in nature, but within the plot of the story, they form an elaborate framework of (slightly paradoxical) rules that determines how vampires can be identified, located and destroyed. The method of their eventual destruction–a stake through the heart–is taken from the folkloristic superstitions quoted by the credulous Calmet but it is notable that in *Dracula* the final disposal of the Count is actually rather anticlimactic; the pleasures of the text are in the chase rather than the kill, and in the way that a slowly-developing understanding of the vampire's nature serves as a guiding thread to draw the characters through the mazy story-line.

The vampires of *Vampire City* can operate by day, and may, in fact, lead apparently normal lives within human society. Their (more-than-slightly paradoxical) vampiric nature is superimposed on a straightforwardly material form, and only becomes glaringly visible when they indulge their nasty habit–although their humanity is further compromised by a certain mechanical quality which likens them to clockwork automata. They are closely associated with various animal analogues, including bats, snakes, vultures and leeches, and are also capable of remarkable metamorphoses, but they are severely allergic to the ashes of their own kind. Their victims do not become vampires in their own right, but are somehow assimilated into their murderers, becoming sub-forms capable of independent manifestation and of "doubling" (thus conferring upon the master vampire the useful capacities of "dividuation" and "alibi-ty"). These vampires too must spend part of each day comatose–and hence vulnerable–actually within rather than merely supported by some relic of their own "homeland." Rather than merely being staked, however, the hearts of Selene's vampires must be surgically excised and burnt while they lie in their shell-like beds (an operation that may only be safely carried out while they are in a weakened state, awaiting "re-winding" by a key applied by an "evil priest" to the hole that every vampire has in his or her chest).

As in *Dracula*, this haphazard patchwork of notions, which overlaps Stoker's at some points and is jarringly discontinuous at others, is integrated into a framework whose gradual revelation allows the characters to negotiate their way through the story to the destruction of their chief enemy and subsequent confrontation with his merely human associates. This contrasts with *The Vampire Countess*, whose unsteady story-line was presumably invented as it went along, and may well have been modified by editorial pressure, and also with *Knightshade*, whose plot was planned in advance as an inescapable maze. Both earlier efforts have obvious merits–the predatory scenes in *The Vampire Countess* are brilliantly vivid, and the placement of the erotically-supercharged confrontation of Addhema and Szandor at the end of the text provides a fine climax, while the Gallandesque nesting of stories within *Knightshade* contrives a remarkable intricacy–but *Vampire City* has more narrative traction and a smoother narrative flow than either of its predecessors, and its parodic analysis of Gothic follies benefits considerably from its orderliness.

The scene in *Vampire City* in which the heart of the comatose Monsieur Goetzi is cut out and incinerated is similar in spirit, if not in fine detail, to the staking scenes in *Dracula*, for reasons that have as much to do with erotic symbolism as folkloristic motifs derived from Calmet. In *Vampire City*, however, the darkly symbolic exorcism scene is immediately followed by the slapstick comedy of Merry Bones' confrontation with the vampire horde. Although Féval's description of his characters' adventure in timestopped Selene has some highly effective melodramatic touches, dramatic suspense is casually dispelled when the interval of suspended animation comes to an end–a pattern repeated when the relatively straight-faced invasion of the Gothic castle dissolves in an increasingly-precipitate rush into a comical chaos that can only be redeemed by a reawakening to sanity. Two points need to be made in respect of these narrative moves which reveal partially-hidden agendas common to both Féval and Stoker.

Although Goetzi and Dracula feature in their respective narratives as unique embodiments of evil who dominate other, merely human, characters and bend them to their will, they are both representative of an entire alien species and an entire social order (if this is less obvious in *Dracula* than *Vampire City*, the modern vampire literature which has proliferated in Dracula's wake has made it abundantly clear). Even though *Vampire City* gives greater prominence the sexual element of vampiric predation than Féval's earlier vampire novels, it certainly does not dispose of its economic and political connotations. Goetzi, the despoiler of maidens, is only just out of his apprenticeship as a vampire, and his symbolic tomb is far less grandiose than those of vampires who have lived among humans as bankers, politicians and military adventurers; he is in essence, an "adolescent" vampire who has not yet perfected the politics of predation.

If *Vampire City* was, indeed, written and serialized in the year implied by the text, 1867, it must have appeared at almost exactly the same time as volume one of Karl Marx's *Das Kapital* (published in that year in Hamburg). The afterword to *The Vampire Countess* points out passages in that book which make use of vampirism in a metaphorical fashion reminiscent of some of the rhetoric of *The Vampire Countess*, and some of these passages seem even more relevant to *Vampire City*. Part 1 of chapter 10 of *Kapital* alleges that "capital is dead labor which, vampire-like, lives only by sucking living labor" and part 2 of the same chapter analyses the usurpation of labor by various proprietors (including among its key examples "a Wallachian boyar"), giving

elaborate consideration to the particular "appetite...[manifest] in the Danubian Principalities." Even
though Marx was living in Paris during the years when
feuilleton fiction was at its most popular, neither the fervently radical Eugène Sue nor the then-freethinking
Féval seems to have been aware of his work, but in some
respects they seem to have been thinking along similar
lines. In *The Vampire Countess* Féval suggested more
than once that the "real" vampire was Paris itself, the
new metropolis whose own life was parasitic on that of
its citizens; *Vampire City* goes further than that, imag-
ining the whole world as a vampire's nest, whose bankers, generals and highly-placed whores (Féval presumably has scheming royal mistresses in mind when he
speaks of "courtesans") have a parallel existence in a
city composed entirely of mausolea, where their true
selves are periodically "rewound" like clocks by "evil
priests."

The manner in which this peculiar motif is introduced into the narrative suggests that it is an entirely
arbitrary invention improvised in order to offer the
story's heroes an opportunity to destroy their nemesis–
but this too has echoes in the work of Marx and other
19th century economists, who were keen to expose and
analyze the quasi-mechanical economic "works" hidden
within–and allegedly fundamental to–sociopolitical sys-
tems. *Vampire City* is, among other things, a symbolic
representation of the world-within-the-world from which
all power, and hence all oppression, extend. Given this,
there may perhaps be more significance than there seems
in the fact that when the time comes to confront the depleted Goetzi in his inner sanctum, neither the middle-
class Midshipman Ned Barton nor the professional surgeon recruited with the task in mind can undertake the

necessary execution; it is done by Merry Bones, the Irish "nailhead" and one-time butcher's boy, while the aristo-cratically-connected "Anna"–to whom Miss 97 always refers, in awed tones, as *She*–merely looks on with scru-pulously academic interest.

There is no Vampire City in *Dracula*, who emerges from the bloodier pages of history as an avatar of Vlad the Impaler who can trace his ancestry back to Attila the Hun–but his first manifestation in England is as a client of lawyers acting as estate-agents; his "invasion" is a matter of buying an obsolete abbey which he intends to use as one of a series of similar bases where his various soil-laden coffins can be installed. In the end, it is nei-ther the scientist van Helsing nor any of the representa-tives of English respectability who stabs Dracula in the heart, but the brash American entrepreneur, who does not employ the carefully-prescribed wooden stake but an icon of Western frontiersmanship: a Bowie knife. There is, so to speak, more than sex at stake here.

A more conspicuous similarity between Féval and Stoker arises from their use of dreams. The seed from which *Dracula* grew was an actual nightmare which formed the basis of the scene where Jonathan Harker is confronted by three avid "vampire brides" but is saved from the immediate draining of his bodily fluids by Dracula. This revelation has, of course, been a gift to amateur psychoanalysts, who have sought its origins in a hypothetical visit to a brothel where Stoker might have contracted syphilis (although there is no evidence that he actually had syphilis, and no evidence that he patronized brothels). This scene bears an obvious resemblance to the hallucinatory scenes in *The Vampire Countess*, but a more important kinship with *Vampire City* might lie in their conspicuous denials that their substance can be dismissed as mere hallucination.

Stoker issues his denials indirectly, but one of the reasons for *Dracula*'s success was the great care he took to embed the substance of his nightmare within a narrative that makes promiscuous use of all the traditional props of narrative realism: fake documents, including diaries and letters, as well as stylistic mannerisms of description and the reportage of dialogue. Féval's approach is very different, and Miss Jebb's fervent denial that Anne Radcliffe's experience was a dream may seem to some readers to be an unconvincing attempt to weasel out of the ignominy of having employed such a hackneyed device to bring the story to a close, but it is worth trying, if only as an intellectual exercise, to examine the implications of taking that claim seriously.

If Anne Radcliffe's journey to Selene was no a dream, what was it? It can only have been an exercise in what would nowadays be called "alternative history"– although Féval would almost certainly have preferred the term *uchronie* (uchronia in English) had he been familiar with the archetypal French examples of Louis-Napoleon Geoffroy's *Napoleon Apocryphe* (1836) and Charles Renouvier's *Uchronie* (1857). In *Vampire City*, as in our world, the accident of the Duke of Wellington's involvement prevents a sequence of events coming to fruition that might have had very different consequences. The young unknown, comparable to a god, interferes– albeit very slightly–with the influence on our world of a parallel world in which the operations of bankers, generals and courtesans are mechanically renewed. In the novel, of course, the influence is benign; Anne Radcliffe becomes a compiler of Gothic plots rather than a victim of one. In the real world, Geoffroy's all-conquering *Na-*

poleon Apocryphe was replaced by the tragic loser of the Battle of Waterloo.

If Anne Radcliffe's journey to Selene was not a dream, even if it is all moonshine, it was an excursion into a world that might have been–which serves to remind us that alternative worlds are not mere dreams, but meaningful phantoms of actions unmade and choices untaken; and that even if our world happens to be devoid of actual vampires, that does not mean that vampires have nothing to teach us, or that we should not listen to their lessons in a realistic frame of mind.

Notes

[1] Féval's French version is "blond imitation", deliberately using the wrong meaning of "fair." His subsequent remark that it would be contrary to the French national character to employ "*blond escamotage*"–which I have rendered as "fair trickery"–presumably accounts for the fact that his own imitation of English Gothic novels is distinctly dark as well as blithely unfair. A detailed account of traceable English pirate editions of Féval's work can be found in the Introduction.

[2] This character is, of course, fictitious but there is a clue to her inspiration in Scott's *Memoir of Mrs Ann Radcliffe*, whose French translation Féval had obviously read. Scott quotes from Ann's 1797 travel book a passage describing Hardwick in Derbyshire, which had been built by Elizabeth, Countess of Shrewsbury. Although the passage does not remark that the lady in question was better known by the nickname "Bess of Hardwick," Féval presumably knew that–hence "Lady B***, du château de Shr***."

[3] Actually, as Féval knew perfectly well–just as he knew how Mrs Radcliffe actually spelled her first name–the Ward family originated in Leicestershire.

[4] William Radcliffe's obituary, quoted verbatim by Scott, records that "[Ann's] maternal grandmother was Anne Oates, the sister of Dr. Samuel Jebb of Stratford, who was the father of Sir Richard." It is the statement that the fictitious Miss Jebb "had now added forty-five years to the [1821] date of Scott's [imaginary] letter" which suggests that Féval–who has already said that all this happened "late last year"–wrote *La Ville-Vampire* in 1867, but I have not been able to trace the serial version in order to confirm that date.

[5] The Ward family actually left London in 1772 and moved to Bath, where Ann might well have encountered Sophia and Harriet Lee.

[6] William Radcliffe's obituary, quoted by Scott, says: "[Ann] was descended from a near relative of the De Witts of Holland. In some family papers which I have seen, it is stated that a De Witt, of the family of John and Cornelius, came to England... bringing with him a daughter, Amelia, then an infant." The Christian name Cornelia is presumably derived from Cornelius, although one of the characters in *A Sicilian Romance* is a nun named Cornelia.

[7] This careful insinuation that the Radcliffes' marriage was not a happy one is utterly gratuitous. Féval surely cannot have known William Radcliffe, although William was, like him, a man trained in law who gave up that vocation to follow another career (as editor of the *English Chronicle*). Perhaps Féval regretted that Scott's memoir remained stubbornly silent regarding the motives of her writing save for the obituary-derived claim that William had encouraged her to begin it when she became bored because his editorial duties so often kept him late at the office. Féval was, of course, far too much of a gentleman to speculate that William might have been so intensely jealous of his wife's literary success that she had to abandon her career to soothe his wounded vanity, and that her detailed pen-portraits of domineering male villains might have drawn inspiration from the well of personal feeling. Even modern critics who would like to establish Ann as a proto-feminist have balked at any such suggestion, although Robert Miles, in *Ann Radcliffe: The Great Enchantress* (1995) does call attention to the unusual fact that the first signature placed on *The Romance of the Forest* was plain "Ann Radcliffe", to which an indication of marital status was only added in later editions. Féval presumably did not know this, nor could he

have known that asthma is a stress-related (and sometimes stress-induced) condition.

[8] This detail is also derived, via Scott, from William's obituary, although the insinuation that Ann's interest in William's translations was occasionally deflected to more inherently-interesting subjects is entirely Féval's.

[9] The name Ragusa was then attached by Western Europeans to the city which is now Dubrovnik in Croatia.

[10] Féval says "Lightfield"; this and other slightly-fudged references to English geography might be intended to satirize the typical geographical infelicities of the English Gothic novel, but there seems little point in duplicating them in an English version of the novel.

[11] Féval's rendering might be more literally translated as "the shires of Stafford and Shrop"–another mild joke, like that cited in note 6.

[12] This is Féval's principal concession to the fact that Ann Radcliffe always provided rational explanations for the supernatural events in her stories, although the much later reference to the Countess Elvina's old Aeolian harps is a more accurate reflection of the author's strategy.

[13] The text has *eupire*, but this is probably a misprint; Féval subsequently uses the more familiar *oupire*, which he had also used in *La Vampire*; for a more extended discussion of his idiosyncratic application of the term, see the second section of the Afterword.

[14] *Jerusalem Delivered–Gerusalemme Liberata* in the original–is an epic poem about the First Crusade by the Spanish writer Tasso (1544-95), first published in 1581. Although the

author repudiated that edition, and rewrote the poem under a different title, most critics prefer the earlier version cited here.

[15] Carniola is the western province of Slovenia.

[16] All the various substances which the mischievous maids give to the little boy are hard liquor. The cherry liqueur maraschino is reportedly at its finest in Dalmatia; rosolio is a sweet cordial made from brandy, sugar and raisins.

[17] Harpagon is a miserly character of Molière's whose name is used in France as we might use Shylock's, as a synonym for "skinflint."

[18] The French call all parrots "Jacquot" much as we call them "Polly"–the presence in the story of a Polly Bird makes it inconvenient to substitute the more familiar word here.

[19] A tartan is a single-masted Mediterranean coaster.

[20] Synovia–*synovie* in French–is the lubricating fluid secreted by the body to facilitate the smooth working of its joints. It seems likely, however, that the ever-innovative Féval, heedless of its pre-existent meaning, synthesized the word from syn–familiar in French, as in English, in such words as synonym and synapse–and vie, intending to imply something like "joined life."

[21] John Hunyadi (1407-1456)–Jean Hunyade in Féval's version–was the scion of a noble Hungarian family who became voivode of Transylvania and Captain of Belgrade, in which capacity he waged war against the Turks. He won a famous victory over Mezid Bey in the last year of his life–the year in which Vlad the Impaler first became ruler of Walachia.

²² Prince Eugene was Eugène de Savoie-Carignan (1663-1736), a son of the Comte de Soissons who entered the service of Austria after being refused an army by Louis XIV and fought the Turks at Zenta in 1697.

²³ Féval's reference to l'académie des Cruches-Cassées could be more literally rendered as "the Academy of Broken Pitchers", but he presumably intended to imply more–or less–than an interest in archaeology.

²⁴ Féval could have used the excuse that it was all a dream to "rationalize" his story–although Ann Radcliffe never stooped so low–but propriety did indeed forbid the use of such a threadbare device. Féval's attempt to wriggle out of his predicament is as implausible as any of Ann Radcliffe's "explanations" for apparent apparitions, but he would not have been unduly troubled by that.

²⁵ Scanderbeg (or Skanderbeg) was the nickname of Georges Castriota (1403-1468), an Albanian prince who won a famous victory over Iskander Bey during the same series of campaigns that made John Hunyadi famous.

²⁶ Féval used the name Johann Spurzheim in *Les Compagnons du Silence* (1857) as an alias of the villainous David Heimer, the machiavellian chief of the secret police of the Kingdom of Naples (who prefigures the infamous Colonel of *Les Habits Noirs*).

CPSIA information can be obtained
at www.ICGtesting.com
Printed in the USA
LVHW031633131122
733045LV00002B/253